An Agent for Madeleine

WESTERN BRIDES UNDERCOVER #4

JO GRAFFORD, WRITING AS JOVIE GRACE

ISBN: 978-1-63907-052-7

Get A Free Book!

Join my mailing list to be the first to know about new releases, free books, special discount prices, Bonus Content, and giveaways.

https://BookHip.com/GNVABPD

Acknowledgments

Thank you so much to my beta readers — Mahasani, J. Sherlock, Auntie Em, and Lady Godiva. Another big thank you goes to my amazing editor, Cathleen Weaver. I am also wildly grateful to my Cuppa Jo Readers on Facebook for reading and loving my books!

About this Series

The Pinkerton National Detective Agency *(established in 1850)* was ahead of its time when it came to hiring women...as well as hunk-a-licious lawmen, wounded soldiers, rugged frontiersmen, and swoon-worthy cowboys. Some were spies. Some got to work under-cover. A few even pretended to be married to their lovely female partners while they were working undercover.

Fortunately for us, agents are required to keep detailed records of their exploits — and in the case of this sweetly suspenseful historical romance series — their accidental attractions, fake relationships, marriages of convenience, stolen kisses, and lassoed hearts.

These are their case files!

Chapter 1: The Pact

MADELEINE

December, 1874

MADELEINE CARUTHERS READ the short letter for at least the hundredth time.

I need your help.

It was from her friend, Jolene. As she slipped it back inside her apron pocket, she knew what she had to do. She'd never really expected this day to come, but a promise was a promise. She was needed in Texas, which meant it was time to pack and say her goodbyes. Thank goodness she had enough money saved up to purchase a train ticket. Just barely.

"Are you finished wool gathering, Miss Caruthers?"

Madeleine's head snapped up at Widow Miller's

sharp tone. "I, ah..." She hastily resumed her task of washing table linens while she debated the best way to announce her upcoming departure. She knew the members of the ladies' auxiliary would immediately start asking questions, but they would be questions she had no answers for. She had no idea how long she would be gone and if she would ever return to Missouri. Not to mention it would take months to save up for another train ticket.

Mercy, but it was cold today! She shivered and glanced over her shoulder at the wood stove, wishing her wash bucket was sitting closer to it. Her fingers felt like ice in the cold, sudsy water. However, Widow Miller always ensured the most senior ladies occupied the spots closest to the stove. The younger church volunteers got to work in whatever space was left — usually the corners of the room that were furthest away from the heat. The only exception to that rule was Widow Miller's daughter, Fannie.

It wasn't fair, of course. Most of the other younger women grumbled about it beneath their breath. Some of them grumbled to each other. Not wishing to give Widow Miller's spoiled, privileged daughter the satisfaction of hearing her complain out loud like the others, Madeleine did all of her grumbling inside her head.

As if reading her thoughts, however, Fannie glanced up from her wash bucket near the stove. Catching Madeleine's eye, she gave a knowing smirk and tossed her chestnut curls over her shoulder.

Madeleine nodded a greeting to the young woman and quickly returned her attention to her own bucket. Hopefully, the temperature outside would warm up a little, because the ladies were cleaning up after yesterday's charity dinner, which meant they had a long day of work ahead of them.

Well, maybe not so long for me. She needed to return to her boarding house room with enough time left to pack her travel bag and walk the short distance to the train depot. The last train for the evening would depart at six o'clock. She planned to be on it.

"I'm not certain what that poor tablecloth ever did wrong to you."

Madeleine jolted at the sound of Fannie's voice. She'd been so lost in thought that she hadn't heard the widow's daughter approach. The trill of mocking laughter that followed Fannie's observation made Madeleine bite her lower lip. She drew a bracing breath to quell her irritation, wishing Fannie didn't try so hard to be a constant burr on her backside. Though she was only two years younger than Madeleine's three and twenty years, she always treated Madeleine like an old spinster rusticating on the proverbial shelf.

"Good morning, Fannie," she murmured, pleased at the bland tone she'd managed to muster. She'd long since learned it was best to simply listen to and lavish compliments on the young woman, rather than make any effort to befriend her.

"Yes, it is a good morning." Fannie gave a twirl,

making her full skirt fan out around her. "I thought you might enjoy a closer look at my new gown."

Madeleine tamped down on a stab of envy as she raised her head. She knew it was wrong to yearn for all the things Fannie had — a mother and a home, not to mention an endless supply of gowns, hats, parasols, ribbons, and shoes.

Like the rest of her wardrobe, Fannie's new dress was stunning. It was made from yards of navy wool fabric. Its gold buttons and gold braiding brought to mind a military uniform. Most importantly, it looked comfortable and warm.

"It's absolutely lovely." Madeleine didn't stop her scrubbing, fully intending to finish her pile of dirty tablecloths in record time. Though she needed to leave the church early, she didn't intend to leave her work there unfinished.

"It's not supposed to look lovely," Fannie wailed. A petulant expression rose to her plump cheeks, making her look downright childish. "It's supposed to look smart and dashing, like the officers coming home for Christmas." Their return was scheduled to take place a week from now. It was the talk of the town, particularly among the single ladies.

"Your gown is both lovely and dashing," Madeleine assured quickly, surprised at how vocal Fannie was being about the return of the Missouri regiment. She'd been under the distinct impression that Fannie was sweet on Pastor Josh Michaelson, the same as she was. Well, maybe not quite the same. Madeleine was convinced that her own feelings for the man ran much deeper than Fannie's. Not that it mattered. He'd shown no romantic interest in either of them. And now that she was leaving town, she'd probably never see him again.

"I reckon that'll do." A hint of a pout remained in Fannie's voice, though she appeared somewhat mollified by the additional compliment Madeleine had given her. "Are you planning on attending the dance in their honor next Friday?"

Madeleine's hands stilled in the water. She supposed now was as good a time as any to share the news that she was leaving. "Most unfortunately, I am not. I'm heading out of town."

"You're leaving? Before Christmas?" Fannie's voice rose in astonishment, causing hands across the room to grow still in their buckets. Heads swiveled in astonishment in their direction.

"I'm afraid so." Madeleine didn't mind the prospect of not having to endure yet another holiday watching Fannie primp, preen, and otherwise monopolize the attentions of every eligible young gentleman in town.

"Where will you go?" the young socialite demanded.

"To Bull County, Texas." Madeleine had never heard of the place. According to her friend, Jolene, it was no more than a tiny speck on the map. Nevertheless, it was where both Jolene and Lorelai were currently residing — her two dearest friends in the world.

She'd met Jolene and Lorelai at the orphanage down the street, where the three of them had been raised together. They were like sisters. No, it was more than that. They were closer than blood. What's more, they'd sworn their allegiance to each other — for life — during a childhood pact. In a nutshell, they'd promised to drop everything and come running if one of them ever asked for help, no questions asked.

So that's what Madeleine was doing.

"What's in Bull County?" Fannie sounded suspicious and a tad condescending.

Madeleine shrugged, since she'd never laid eyes on the town. "Not much, from what I hear, other than a friend in need."

"A friend, eh?" Fannie's clever mind quickly connected the dots. "You're not, by any chance, referring to one of those girls from the orphanage?"

Madeleine was saved from having to answer the question by the crowd of lady auxiliary members who descended on her.

"I am going to miss you!" Mrs. Albright reached her first and enclosed her in a pair of scrawny, bird-like arms. "How long will you be gone, child?" She was a sprightly little woman who always smelled like cinnamon and sugar. When she wasn't volunteering at the church, she could be found baking pies, tarts, puddings, and cakes.

"I'm not certain." Madeleine wished she could tell

her more. Mrs. Albright had always been kind to her, bringing her homemade soup when she'd come down with a cold last winter. She'd additionally always made sure Madeleine was among the recipients of the coats and gloves that got donated to the church each Christmas. By leaving town before Christmas, Madeleine was going to miss out on such generosity this year, but it couldn't be helped. She could only hope that her current threadbare coat had another season of wear in it.

"Will you at least promise to write?" Mrs. Albright gave her a final squeeze and let her go so that the next woman in line could crowd in for a hug.

"I will." Madeleine found herself blinking back tears. Her life in Missouri hadn't been easy. Nevertheless, Missouri was home, the only one she'd ever known. The thought of leaving its familiar rolling hills behind was a little depressing. Someone stuffed a handkerchief in her hand. She lifted it to dab at her eyes.

Truth be told, there was one person in particular she was dreading parting with the most. It was a foolish sentiment, since Pastor Josh Michaelson probably wouldn't even notice she was missing from his congregation.

"Good morning, ladies," a cheerful male voice boomed, interrupting her melancholy thoughts.

She froze as the very man she'd been thinking about stepped into the fellowship hall. Not wishing to be seen by him in her faded gray work dress and thread-bare apron, she made an effort to hunker down within the small crowd of church ladies. As a further precaution, she thrust her red and water-shriveled hands behind her back. It was way too bad her name happened to be the current topic of discussion, but maybe she would be fortunate enough to escape his notice.

"I appreciate all that the auxiliary is doing to get this place whipped back into shape."

Madeleine peeked around the head of the lady who'd just finished hugging her, watching him scan the room with his coffee-brown eyes. His expression quickly transitioned from appreciation to puzzlement as he noted the number of ladies absent from their workstations.

"Is everything alright in here?" A concerned frown settled across his high, aristocratic forehead.

"Not exactly," Mrs. Albright sighed, tucking a loose strand of gray hair back into her normally tidy bun.

To Madeleine's dismay, she pointed in her direction. "We just found out that Madeleine is leaving town."

"Indeed?" Pastor Josh Michaelson's voice was low without inflection. His dark gaze followed where Mrs. Albright pointed.

Madeleine immediately experienced the jolt she felt every time their gazes met. Because she'd spent so many months hiding her feelings for him, perfecting (she hoped) a look of sublime indifference, she could easily recognize when another person was doing the same thing.

The realization shook her. Unless she was losing her mind, there was only one explanation for the thinly masked disappointment in the eyes of the tall, dark, and heart-meltingly handsome pastor. He was not indifferent to her. She was certain of it, though he'd never been anything other than impeccably professional in her presence.

It was the same way he treated every other member of their church congregation. From what she could glean, Pastor Michaelson didn't attend parties or socialize with any of the eligible young ladies in town — and not from a lack of interest on their part. They smiled, simpered, and flirted in his direction, but nothing had ever come of it. The townsfolk often remarked what a pity it was that the young minister acted like he was married to the work of the Lord. It was generally understood that, short of a miracle, their priestly pastor would remain unwed.

Madeleine could only hope there was nothing in her own eyes and demeanor this morning that hinted at how much her heart was pounding at the sight of the confirmed bachelor. He looked every inch a pastor in his somber black suit and overcoat. His thick, blue-black hair was a bit tousled, as if he'd just come inside from the winter breeze, and his black top hat was gripped in one hand at his side. He never bothered carrying a walking stick like so many of the fashionable young men favored.

"Yes, indeed, pastor!" Mrs. Albright wiped her eyes. "She's headed for the wild west, a place teaming with lawlessness and heathens." Her voice grew fierce. "We should say a special prayer over her for traveling mercies, don't you agree?"

"I do, ma'am."

They were three simple words, but they filled Madeleine with dread. His answer indicated that she would soon be standing face-to-face with the man she'd been madly in love with for an entire year.

"If you'd be so kind as to step forward, Miss Caruthers." Josh Michaelson tossed his hat on the nearest table and unbuttoned his overcoat. He shrugged out of it and laid it across the back of one of the chairs. Reaching into the pocket of his trousers, he withdrew a small glass vial of olive oil.

Drawing a deep breath and silently praying for composure, Madeleine glided in his direction on legs that trembled.

He towered several inches over her. As he gazed down at her for the briefest of moments, regret flashed across his tanned features. It was gone so quickly that Madeleine was left wondering if she'd imagined it.

"From the looks of those gathered, you're going to be greatly missed, Miss Caruthers." His baritone voice resounded through her, stirring emotions she didn't dare explore too deeply.

"Thank you, pastor," she intoned softly. There was a faint tremor to her voice, but it could easily be explained by the tearful parting between females that he'd interrupted. There was no reason for him to presume he was the cause of her emotional state, though she knew he was most assuredly a part of it.

He nodded, his expression returning to its normal pastorly politeness. "With your permission, Miss Caruthers, I'm going to place a dot of oil on your forehead. Then I'm going to pray with you. I have no doubt that, as a woman of faith, you understand there are no supernatural qualities vested in the oil itself. It's merely symbolic of the anointing power of our heavenly Father."

She nodded her approval. She'd always appreciated his down-to-earth approach to religion. He was genuine and real, not given to pompous posturing and hoodoo voodoo antics like so many of the ministers who'd visited the orphanage. She'd been forced to endure their sermons under the threat of punishment if she and her friends had so much as whispered or wiggled during them.

Without any further ado, Pastor Michaelson uncapped the vial of oil, tipped it to coat his finger, and gently traced a cross on Madeleine's forehead.

Then he laid the glass vial on a nearby table and reached out to lightly rest his hands on her shoulders.

"Our heavenly Father." He prayed in the same low and eloquent voice he used for regular conversations. There was no singsong chanting, nothing but unwavering confidence in a Creator who had ears to hear without any unnecessary embellishments. "Be with our friend, Madeleine Caruthers, as she travels. I ask that You protect her every mile of her journey. Give her comfort in the absence of her friends. Give her wisdom to direct her decisions in the coming days. All this I ask in the name of a Savior who cares about us all — every child, every widow, and every orphan. Amen."

Madeleine was so moved by the prayer that a few extra heartbeats passed before she opened her eyes. She felt Josh Michaelson's hands leave her shoulders and immediately missed the warmth of them. For a man who'd not once lavished any personal attention on her during his one-year tenure at the church, he seemed very well versed about her circumstances. He clearly knew that she was an orphan. Despite her humble background, he also seemed to have gone out of his way during his prayer to assure her that she mattered in the Kingdom of Heaven.

As she raised her head and met his dark, searching gaze, she couldn't help wondering if she mattered to him, as well — in any way, no matter how small. Did she ever cross his mind after hours when his church business was concluded? Did he ever daydream about her the way she daydreamed about him? Did he ever wish for the opportunity to get to know her better, the way she'd always longed to get to know him?

A sudden silence settled across their gathering. Biting her lower lip, Madeleine hurried to end it before it grew awkward. "Thank you, pastor." She inclined her head graciously.

"You are most welcome, Miss Caruthers." He clasped his hands in front of him, not seeming in any hurry to end their encounter. "If you don't mind me asking, where exactly will you be heading?"

She offered what she hoped was a friendly smile, devoid of anything more than politeness. "To Bull County, Texas. It's a very small community. I doubt you've heard of it."

A thoughtful frown rippled across his forehead. "As it turns out, I have." He reached for his hat and overcoat, draping it over one arm. "It's near the town called Midland Hills, where a business associate of mine resides."

"Have you visited there, sir?" Madeleine's heart-beat sped with hope. The discovery that he had a friend living near Bull County made her destination no longer feel so far away from, well...*him*.

It seemed to her that he hesitated before answering. "I have not, but I hope to visit him in the near future." The benign smile he'd been wearing up to this point was gone. His dark eyes raked across her features, making her feel like he was probing for answers to questions not yet asked. "When do you plan to depart, Miss Caruthers?"

His abrupt question caught her off guard. Though she didn't understand why it mattered to him, she was unaccountably delighted that it did. "This evening, pastor. I plan to catch the six o'clock train."

"Do you have a ride to the train station?"

Her eyes widened at his continued interrogation. Of course, she didn't have a ride! Women in her economic circumstances walked everywhere.

Somewhere in the distance, Fannie gave a titter of mirth. Madeleine's face burned with mortification at the sound. "The good Lord gave me two feet capable of getting me to where I need to go, sir." Her voice came out more tart than she intended, which was entirely Fannie's fault.

His dark gaze flickered past her head with a hint of irritation before returning to her. "He certainly did, ma'am, but there's a snow storm brewing, and I happen to have a buggy rented for the afternoon. I'd be much obliged if you'd allow me to drive you to the station, thereby ensuring your safe arrival." He frowned in contemplation at her. "That is, if you don't mind arriving a few hours early."

She was so astounded by his offer that she hardly knew how to respond.

In the end, Mrs. Albright made the decision for her. "Of course, she'd appreciate the ride, pastor. I'll come along to chaperone and keep things right and proper."

At Widow Miller's gasp of outrage, Mrs. Albright waved one wiry arm. "No, this is not merely an attempt to get out of work. Despite the fact that my joints have been acting up something awful lately, I'll be back in plenty of time to do my share of the washing."

Without waiting for a response, she reached for Madeleine's elbow and towed her from the room behind Pastor Michaelson. He paused with a gallant flourish at the coat closet in the front foyer, allowing them a moment to retrieve their hats, coats, and gloves.

Madeleine turned to survey the beautiful sanctuary one last time. The cold winter sun was shining through the stained glass windows, casting multi-hued splashes of light and color across the pews. On the distant platform, the knotty oak pulpit stood empty and ready for Josh Michaelson's tall frame to stand behind it. Sadly, she wouldn't be there next Sunday to see him.

Moments later, he was lifting her and Mrs. Albright into the buggy. She ended up in the middle of the bench, sandwiched between the two of them. Mrs. Albright started to hum some hymn or another off-tune. Her head was turned away from them, gazing at the bare trees and plank storefronts lining 5th Avenue. Oddly enough, her behavior gave Madeleine and Pastor Michaelson some modicum of privacy in which to converse.

He wasted no time lifting the horses' reins and picking up where their previous conversation had left off.

"I presume you have friends in Bull County, Miss Caruthers?"

"Two," she confirmed happily. They hit a bump in the road, which caused his knee to knock against hers. She suppressed a shiver of awareness. "Both are from here. You might have heard of them. Lorelai Woods and Jolene Lilygate." Not that he needed or wanted to hear her life story, but she added a trifle breathlessly, "We grew up together at the orphanage."

To her surprise and disappointment, his expression became grave. Instead of answering, he fell silent.

Anxious to keep the conversation between them going, Madeleine gave a self-deprecatory chuckle. "Actually, I keep forgetting both of them are married now, so their last names have changed."

"To what?" His tone was so clipped that she blinked.

"Lorelai Langston and Jolene Barella."

He coughed and cleared his throat. "What do their husbands do for a living?"

She turned her head to frown up at him. Why in heaven's name did he care about the occupations of her friends' husbands? This was far from the conversation she'd spent the last year dreaming of having with him. "Lorelai is married to a gentleman rancher, and Jolene wed a handyman employed at the boarding house." Madeleine would have much preferred to talk about something involving Pastor Michaelson's life — preferably what he meant about potentially visiting Bull County soon. Would their paths cross when he did? Now *that* was something worth discussing!

"Please. Don't go." Josh Michaelson spoke in such a low voice that Madeleine wondered if he intended for her to hear his plea.

"I beg your pardon, sir?" She glanced furtively in Mrs. Albright's direction. Fortunately, the dear soul still appeared to be paying them no mind.

"I didn't want to say anything in front of the others at church, but..." He, too, glanced in Mrs.

Albright's direction before returning his attention to Madeleine.

She caught her breath at the stark concern etched across his features. She could barely breathe while she waited for him to elaborate. Though she didn't understand the source of his worry, she was thrilled that he was no longer acting formal or indifferent to her.

"It's dangerous down there." He nosed his buggy in front of the boarding house where she was currently staying. It was a clapboard building that had once been painted white. Its walls had long since become weathered and dingy from the wind and rain.

She peeked at him from beneath her lashes to gauge his response to the humble abode. He was frowning so ferociously at the reins in his hands that it was impossible to tell what he thought of the building they were parked in front of.

The first tendrils of anxiety curled in her gut. "What kind of danger?" she prodded.

"It's infested with cattle rustlers and highway robbers, that's what." Instead of hopping down to assist her from the buggy, Josh Michaelson twisted impulsively in her direction. "Miss Caruthers, I really don't care for the idea of you traveling alone to such a lawless part of the country. Is there anything I can do to talk you out of it?"

The agony in his eyes was so real that it made Madeleine's breathing hitch. She badly wanted to say something that would bring a smile back to his mouth that was pressed into a thin, hard line. However, her integrity wouldn't allow it. She had precious few things in the world to offer anyone. She had little money and few possessions. But she'd given her word to a friend, and her word was good.

"No, sir," she returned simply. "I made a promise to a friend in need, and I plan to keep it."

His face paled a few degrees. Leaping down from the driver's seat, he reached for her. Setting her feet carefully on the ground, his gaze locked on hers again. "I'll wait for you here."

Her heart thumped at the conflicting emotions warring their way across the harsh lines of his cheekbones and the jut of his jaw. "Thank you, sir. I won't be long."

She could feel his eyes burning into her shoulder blades as she hurried inside the boarding house. She wasn't jesting when she'd said it wouldn't take her long to pack. She owned little more than a spare gown, one ragged quilt, and a handful of books, all of which she swiftly tossed inside the faded travel bag she'd acquired second-hand. Then there was her tiny sewing basket, a minimal number of toiletries, stationery, and ink. After a quick mental debate, she decided to leave her lantern behind. There was no easy way to transport it without breaking the glass or spilling the oil. Neither were risks she wanted to take.

Before she left the building, she stopped at the front desk to notify them of her departure and pay her final bill. She couldn't afford to continue paying rent while she was away.

Pastor Josh Michaelson was waiting for her outside, as promised. He wordlessly reached for her travel bag and secured it to the back of the buggy. Then he lifted her back into the seat next to Mrs. Albright. Climbing in beside her, he resumed their drive to the train station in rigid silence.

Madeleine rode next to him in misery, hating to part from him like this. Disapproval was rolling off him in nearly tangible waves.

Mrs. Albright continued to hum off-key, but she occasionally cast a sympathetic glance in Madeleine's direction.

When they arrived at the train station, Pastor Michaelson wasted no time in assisting Madeleine to the ground and handing over her travel bag. Then he stood for a moment, gazing down at her with an inscrutable expression.

"I am sorry you disapprove of what I'm doing," she burst out, no longer able to endure his censure.

He glared at her. "I don't disapprove of you, Miss Caruthers. I'm simply worried about you."

"Then stop. Please." Though it wasn't his place to worry about her, his words struck a thrilling chord. She bit her lower lip, hardly knowing what else to say.

He shook his head and glanced away, scrubbing his hand over the lower half of his face. "If I could rearrange my schedule on such short notice, I'd escort you there myself."

"Pastor Michaelson," she gasped. It seemed to her that, somewhere in their conversation, they'd crossed a line. Whatever was happening between them felt much more personal now.

He wrenched his gaze back to hers. "Since I am not in the position to ensure your safety, Miss Caruthers, be assured I will pray for you every day that you're away."

Her breath came out in a damp expulsion. Sadly, she would not be returning to Missouri any time soon, if at all. At some point, he would realize that. Would he cease praying for her then? The thought made her want to weep. Pastor Josh Michaelson was finally looking at her like a man who saw her as a woman — not as simply another face in his congregation.

It was way too bad it had taken her imminent departure from town to earn such regard.

"Thank you," she choked, blinking rapidly. "Thank you for the ride, for your kindness, for everything, sir." This was goodbye. Her heart ached from the necessity of leaving him, possibly for good.

He nodded, still holding her gaze. A vein ticked in his neck. He reached out as if to touch her hand, but he let his arm drop without making contact. "May the Lord go with you, Miss Caruthers."

Wrenching his gaze away from hers at long last, he leaped into the buggy and drove away without looking back.

Chapter 2: The Summons

JOSH

JOSH FOUND it difficult to concentrate on his sermon the next morning. He was too busy chastising himself for not doing more to prevent Madeleine Caruthers from leaving town. She'd been sitting in his congregation for an entire year — over there on the right side, second row back, in the seat nearest the aisle.

It was not going to be the same, pastoring a church without her splash of white-blonde hair in the congregation in front of him. It didn't matter that she wore the same faded navy dress every Sunday or that her boots were scuffed. To him, she still stood out like a peacock among doves. A princess among paupers. An angel among mere mortals. She was truly that beautiful — so beautiful that he couldn't believe she remained unwed. What was wrong with the young bucks in town? Couldn't they see she was worth a hundred of those silly, frivolous creatures like Fannie Miller and her bevy of empty-headed friends? Young women who cared for little more than the next gown they would purchase or the next set of ribbons they would tie in their hair.

Madeleine had so much more substance to her. She tutored the young girls at the orphanage in arithmetic and geography. Evenings and weekends, she took in washing and mending. Despite all of that, she somehow still found time to serve in the ladies' auxiliary. Rumor had it she was also one of the regular visitors to the eldest members of their congregation, shut-ins who were no longer able to attend church services.

In all honesty, she would have made the perfect pastor's wife. Madeleine Caruthers, quite simply, was everything Josh had ever dreamed of. Unfortunately, he wasn't free to court, much less marry.

As he was delivering his final remarks, movement in the back of the church caught his attention. The door opened and closed, and a small lad sidled inside. He was one of the street urchins who liked to linger outside the church sometimes. Usually, he was looking for a handout. Josh gave him a coin now and then. Yesterday, he'd been able to feed the little fellow with leftovers from the charity dinner. Not once in Josh's memory, however, had he been bold enough to step inside the church building. He hoped the lad's presence didn't indicate something was wrong — something he intended to find out as soon as the service ended.

Forcing his attention back to the congregation, Josh gave a prayer to conclude the service. Then he spoke a blessing over the congregation. Sometimes, he composed new and catchy words of wisdom, hoping to send the church members back to their regular lives with a whimsical smile on their faces. Today, he fell back on a tried-and-true passage from the Book of Numbers:

> *"May the Lord bless you*
> *And keep you;*
> *May the Lord make his face shine*
>   *on you*
> *And be gracious to you;*
> *May the Lord turn his face toward you*
> *And give you peace."*

He could only hope that he would be able to find such peace in the next few days. It was unlikely, though, while he was busy worrying about the danger Madeleine's train might be hurtling her toward.

The usual cluster of church members filled the center aisle as he slowly worked his way toward the street urchin in the back of the building. If his memory served, the boy's name was Luke.

"Good morning, Pastor Michaelson!" Fannie Miller stepped directly in his path to deliver a well-practiced curtsey. Though her pale gold gown was lovely, her actions reeked of pretentiousness.

"Good morning, Miss Miller." He inclined his head with as much politeness as he could muster and stepped around her.

"I enjoyed your sermon, sir," she called after him, sounding a bit miffed. No doubt she would have preferred their conversation to last longer.

"Thank you, Miss Miller." Though he knew his actions were bordering on rudeness, he didn't give her more than a glance over his shoulder. "Pardon my haste, ma'am, but we have a visitor requiring my attention."

Her gaze had already lighted on Luke, and her upturned nose was wrinkled in distaste.

Swallowing his irritation at her inability to hide her disdain for the less fortunate, he hurried up to the young fellow. "Master Luke! How are you, sir?" He rendered him a mock salute.

The boy grinned at the pompous greeting, understanding it for the jest it was meant to be. He proudly saluted back, sticking out his skinny chest. "I gotta message for ya, pastor." He rummaged in his pocket and fished out a much-bedraggled telegram. Instead of handing it straight over, however, he held out his hand in desperate need of washing. Dirt was caked beneath his fingernails.

"It's going to cost me, eh?" Shaking his head and grinning, Josh reached into his pocket for a coin. "I reckon this means there are no discounts for pastors, even on a Sunday morning?"

"Well, now..." Luke ran a hand through his filthy hair, making the uncombed red locks stick out in all directions. "Ya see here, pastor, the telegraph office is closed on Sundays, so this 'ere is an extra special deliv'ry."

"Ah, so it's going to cost me extra." Josh's grin widened. He handed over two coins instead of one.

As his fingers closed around the money, the lad flashed Josh such a grateful look that it twisted his insides.

"If you come back in the morning, I'll see about replacing those boots, too." He nodded at the boy's feet. Both boots were sporting holes in the toes. According to Mrs. Albright, the church was expecting some clothing donations from Farmer Mike's family tomorrow, and Mike had a couple of boys. More than likely, there'd be some boots to spare. If not, Josh planned to march Luke straight to a cobbler and have a pair custom made. He couldn't stand the thought of the lad suffering frostbite from the winter temperatures.

Luke stared at him for a moment. Then he gave a low whistle. "I shore will, pastor. Much obliged." He shook his head. "Ain't nobody around 'ere ever gave a rip the way you do." With that, he slapped the telegram in Josh's hand, tipped his cap, and took off at a jog.

Widow Miller, who'd just ambled her way up the aisle, gave a small yelp of protest. "No running in church, lad! No running, I say!"

Luke glanced over his shoulder as he twisted the door handle open. His upper lip was curled in rebellion.

Josh gave him a wink and another salute, earning an outraged gasp from Mrs. Miller.

"I declare you encourage that little scamp way too much," she chided.

For the life of him, Josh couldn't fathom what else anyone would expect of a pastor than to encourage and inspire others. However, he let her statement go without comment. He was too anxious to return to his office and read the contents of the mysterious telegram. The very fact that someone had hired a courier, albeit a short and humbly dressed one, to deliver it to him on a Sunday, told him that it was important. He wouldn't be surprised if turned out to be a message from his superiors — not the church officials from their home office in Springfield, but from the Pinkerton National Detective Agency in St. Louis.

The agency was the real reason he had no time or place in his life for romance. He was truly an ordained minister; there was nothing fake about his license to preach. However, he had a second vocation, a far more dangerous one — that of a Pinkerton agent.

He was working undercover right now, investigating a set of arson cases across the midwest states that had baffled the authorities for the past two years. In the past month alone, he and his fellow agents had succeeded in uncovering a ring of dissatisfied factory workers who'd taken to burning down office buildings in order to collect the insurance money. Several arrests had been made, and they were close to wrapping up the case.

Inevitably, that meant the powers-that-be at the Pinkerton Agency would be sending him a new assignment soon. Did the telegram that Luke had delivered contain that new assignment?

Josh marched back down the church aisle, greeting several more members of the congregation on his way to his office behind the platform. Once seated at his roll-top desk, he eagerly unfolded the slip of paper.

Need you in Bull County, Texas immediately. STOP Replacement pastor on the way. STOP Permanent relocation.

The telegram was time-stamped at the close of business yesterday. Saturday at six o'clock in the evening, to be precise. Josh dropped it on his desk, a dozen torrid emotions swirling through his brain. For one thing, his new assignment meant he was heading in the same direction as Madeleine Caruthers, which both thrilled him and filled him with apprehension. Secondly, it meant he'd barely missed the opportunity to escort her to Texas as he'd longed to do. Of all the rotten luck to receive the telegram seventeen hours too late to make that happen!

Thirdly, and even more worrisome, was the fact that Madeleine was going to visit her dearest friends in the world, both of whom just happened to be married to Pinkerton agents. That couldn't be a coincidence. Josh had completed his initial training with Agent Edgar Barella at the home office; and he'd heard about, though never met, Agent John Langston. *Shoot!* Every detective in the agency had heard about John

Langston. To Josh's knowledge, the man was the first and only former pirate to ever join their hallowed ranks.

If he was a betting man, which he wasn't, he'd be willing to wager that since Lorelai and Jolene were now married to these two particular men, it meant they'd been recruited to serve alongside them as female agents.

He didn't know what that spelled in terms of their summons to Madeleine, but he had his suspicions. Dark, ugly, dreadful suspicions! As much as he didn't want to think about it, there was a distinct possibility she was being recruited to become a Pinkerton agent, as well.

No! He leaned his elbows on his desk and dropped his head into his hands. *Please, no!* She was too soft and feminine, too demure, too kindhearted, and too blasted sweet. The life of an undercover detective was not the kind of life for a gentle creature like her. She deserved a home with a cheerful kitchen and a fire in the hearth. She deserved...

He fisted his hands in his hair. She deserved all the things he'd wanted to give her, but had never been at the liberty to give her due to his job. His second job. The one few people in the world knew anything about.

Then again, maybe he was jumping to conclusions. He smoothed his hair down and leaned back in his chair to read the telegram a second time.

He wracked his brain, trying to remember exactly what Madeleine had said about her reasons for traveling to Bull County. She'd mentioned something about keeping a promise to a friend in need. It had sounded innocuous at the time. Now that he'd received an order to report there for his next assignment, however, he feared there might be more to her friends' summons — much, much more.

No. Upon further reflection, he didn't feel it was likely he was simply jumping to conclusions. Madeleine was heading to a town infested with Pinkerton agents, which meant something big was about to go down there. The fact that Josh was additionally being brought in on the case was further proof to support that theory. He was a highly seasoned agent, one with a plethora of closed cases under his belt.

He stood and started opening and closing desk drawers to remove the few items he needed to take with him. Most of the regular office supplies he would leave behind for the next pastor.

His orders had been clear. He was needed in Bull County, Texas immediately, which meant he was going to have to catch the very next train out of town. His orders also stated that he wasn't supposed to linger until his replacement arrived. He'd learned years ago not to question such orders. There were usually good reasons for a hasty departure from one's current duty station, followed by a shot-gun arrival to the next. Those reasons generally entailed saving lives.

The thing Josh regretted the most about making such an abrupt exit from town was his promise only minutes earlier to young Luke. He'd fully intended to ensure the lad received a new pair of boots. His mind raced over his options. An idea popped into his mind that had him springing for the door.

He rushed out to the quickly emptying sanctuary and was relieved to see Mrs. Albright ambling between the pews, collecting song books. The sight of her made him smile. For reasons he'd never understood, she'd always insisted on collecting the song books and putting them away for the week. If it was up to him, he'd have just left them out for the next Sunday service. The best he could gather was that the song books had always been put away during the week days at this particular church. Leaving them out "simply wasn't done."

The only other person in the building was old Zeke McCoy, who was scraping the coals out of the wood stove in the back of the sanctuary. He nodded at Josh as he stooped to deposit the last of the glowing embers into a metal bucket. The man was a kind-hearted creature, performing all sorts of menial tasks around the church so that Josh wouldn't have to. He'd been scraping coals ever since Josh had presided over the funeral ceremony for his late wife eight months earlier.

"Thank you, Zeke," Josh called, wishing he was at liberty to give the fellow a proper farewell. Zeke was someone he was truly going to miss.

"My pleasure," the aging farmer shot back. He hitched up one of his suspenders and shuffled his way to the door.

"Why, there you are, pastor!" Mrs. Albright

straightened between the pews and shot him a smile full of sunshine. "I wondered where you'd gotten off to."

He shot her a rueful smile at her tactful reference to the way he'd disappeared sooner than usual. Normally, he remained in the sanctuary, shaking hands until the last church member made their exit.

"Please forgive my absence, ma'am. I'm afraid I have some unfortunate news."

"Oh?" With a look of concern, she set her stack of song books down on the nearest pew and hurried across the room to stand in front of him. "What can I do to help?"

"I just received a summons from a sick family member," he lied, hating the necessity of spinning a falsehood. "I'll be leaving town in the morning, and I don't know when I'll be able to return." *Never, most likely.* In the eight years he'd served as a Pinkerton agent, he'd not once been sent back to any town where he'd previously served. Though he'd never precisely been told it was against company policy, he knew it was unlikely due to the undercover nature of their work.

"Oh, my dear man!" Mrs. Albright crooned. A world of sympathy infused her voice. "I am so sorry to hear it."

"The church will be sending a replacement to cover my duties while I am away."

Her expression grew sad. She was one of those rare people who possessed the uncanny ability to read between the lines. On some level, she probably understood he meant he wasn't coming back.

"I would be most grateful to take you up on your offer to help, though," he continued smoothly.

Her blue-gray eyes brightened with hope. "Anything, pastor."

"The street urchin, who likes to hang around, needs a pair of boots. I instructed him to stop back by the church in the morning."

She bobbed her head with energy. "We have a donation coming from Farmer Mike's family. It should be here by then."

"I was hoping you'd say that." He dug in his pocket for a few dollar bills. "If there are no boots to be had in his size, however, I need you to promise me you'll march Luke to the cobbler and have a pair made."

"You can count on it, pastor." She accepted the bills, looking a little awed at the amount he was handing over.

"Maybe you can make sure he receives a meal, now and then, also? It's supposed to be a long winter."

Her gaze softened. "Well, now, you know how my joints have been bothering me something awful. I reckon I could hire him to do a few chores around the house."

Josh Michaelson held out his hand. "I'd be eternally grateful, ma'am."

Her eyes glinted with unshed tears as she clasped it

between both of her hands. "I'm going to miss you, pastor."

"I shall miss you as well, ma'am." After they shook, she seemed in no hurry to let his hand go. "It's been my greatest pleasure serving alongside you," he added gently.

———

HE WAS first in line at the ticket counter when the train station opened the next morning. Since he'd been working two jobs over the past several years, he'd been earning double wages. That meant he could well afford the cost of a ticket for a Pullman sleeper car. Traveling in style was one of the perks of his somewhat nomadic lifestyle. When a man never put down roots or had to buy a house and buggy, it left him with plenty of funds to spend on other conveniences. Though he wasn't one to waste money, he considered a week on a train to be worth the upgrade to a more comfortable set of accommodations.

Instead of contemplating his next assignment like he normally would have, he found himself spending most of his journey west thinking about Madeleine Caruthers. He wondered what her reaction would be when he popped unexpectedly into the same town she was visiting. Would she be half as glad to see him as he was to see her?

He'd mentally replayed their last encounter dozens of times, glorying in the fact that he'd finally gotten her alone for a few minutes in his rented buggy the other day. Well, almost alone. Mrs. Albright had come along to keep things respectable. She'd allowed them to converse uninterrupted, though, for which he was truly grateful.

He relived how it had felt to rest his hands on Madeleine's trim waistline while he lifted her in and out of her seat. He'd never forget the way her blue eyes had gone all wide, soft, and vulnerable in those moments as they clung trustingly to his face, nor how it had felt to have her sitting beside him afterward. Oh, how badly he'd wanted their encounter to mean something more than a simple drive to a train station! He'd almost given in to the weakness of his hopeless attraction to her and said something along those lines before they'd parted ways. He'd reached for her hand without thinking, and only stopped himself in the nick of time before making a complete fool of himself.

He tipped his head back against the train seat and closed his eyes, remembering how their knees and elbows had brushed a few times. She'd smelled good, too, all clean and flowery and feminine. It was a dangerous place for a man in his position to allow his mind to go, but there wasn't much else to do on a long train ride. Once, when he dozed off, he even dreamt he was back in that buggy with Madeleine Caruthers at his side. This time, however, they were alone without a chaperone, and he was leaning closer to brush his mouth against her warm, sweet lips.

Great balls of fire! Josh awoke with a jolt and sat

up. He was a church pastor and a Pinkerton agent, for crying out loud! He had no business either dreaming or daydreaming about kissing a woman like Madeleine. In an effort to clear his mind and focus on the coming case, he borrowed a newspaper and read every article in it from cover to cover. When he was finished, he dozed off again.

The face and form of the delectable Madeleine Caruthers returned to further torment his dreams.

Chapter 3: New Recruit

MADELEINE

One week later

MADELEINE COULD HARDLY CONTAIN her excitement when one of the porters announced that they were due to arrive in Midland Hills in under an hour. She was all cramped, wrinkled, and travel weary and couldn't wait to have her feet back on solid ground. Even more, she couldn't wait to see her friends again.

Midland Hills was the closest town to Bull County that possessed a train station. She'd have to travel by wagon the rest of the way. It was difficult to tell from Jolene's letter, but she very much hoped that Jolene and her husband were planning on meeting her in Midland Hills to save the expense of hiring more transportation. Her friend understood how tight Madeleine's funds were. Now that Madeleine was thinking about it, it was a little strange that they hadn't addressed the matter in writing prior to beginning her journey.

The train whistled its way into the station, and she was soon stretching her legs on the train platform. Swinging her travel bag at her side, she glanced around hopefully. Her heart sank when she failed to catch sight of Jolene.

Oh, dear! She was truly on her own.

On the bright side, it was warmer in Texas than it had been in Missouri. The sun poured down from overhead, enveloping her in warm, dry heat. If she had to venture a guess, the noon day temperatures were nigh on close to eighty degrees. *Glory be!* For a woman wearing threadbare clothing, it was a welcome reprieve from the frost and snow she'd left behind in the midwest.

As the platform started to clear, she scoured the road for any rig that looked like it might be available for hire.

"Miss Caruthers?"

She glanced up to discover a tall, dark-headed man approaching her. Though his brown suit was decent enough, he wore a Stetson instead of a top hat and boots instead of dress shoes. The most worrisome detail of all was that she'd never laid eyes on him in her life.

She pinned him with her best no-nonsense look, hoping he couldn't tell how apprehensive she was. "How did you know my na—?"

"I am Agent Garen Evans, ma'am." He spoke in a

low, well-modulated voice, as if he intended for her to be the only one to hear him. Thrusting out a hand, he lowered his voice a few more notches and added, "I work for the Pinkerton Agency, the same as your friends, Jolene Barella and Lorelai Langston."

She mechanically shook his hand, trying to process his shocking announcement. She'd read about the Pinkertons in the newspaper once, so she knew they were a detective agency. However, she was entirely unprepared to hear that both of her dearest friends in the world were now employed by them. When? How? Why?

Only when Garen Evans was standing directly in front of her did he open the lapel of his suit coat to flash his Pinkerton badge at her. "I'm about to hand you a letter from Jolene. Hopefully, it will answer enough of your questions to convince you it's safe to follow me to my office." He produced a white envelope and handed it to her.

He was right about one thing. She was full of questions. "Why isn't she here to greet me?" She had to set down her travel bag to tear open the envelope. It made no sense that her friend would not deliver the message in person. They were closer than sisters, and it had been a very long time since they'd last seen each other. It only made sense that Jolene would jump at the chance to be reunited. Unless something bad had befallen her...

Madeleine's heart pounded with dread at the recollection that Jolene had stated in her last letter that she was in need of help.

Agent Evans angled his head at the slip of paper she was unfolding. "Just read the letter, ma'am."

Nodding and swallowing hard, she scanned the first few lines.

My dearest Madeleine,

I can only imagine the questions running through your head right now. First and foremost, Lorelai and I are safe. I don't know how much she has shared with you yet, but she is in the family way, and the babe is safe, too.

A sound of surprise escaped Madeleine. *A baby?* No, Lorelai had most certainly told her nothing of the sort. Why? Why so much secrecy? Once upon a time, the three friends would have told each other everything! Madeleine greedily continued reading.

Both Lorelai and I are employed by the Pinkerton National Detective Agency. There is so much we've been wanting to share with you, which we were not at liberty to do until now. Please forgive us for the sleight-of-hand tactics in getting you to join us in Texas, but we truly do need your help. That part of our summons was no exaggeration. The case we're working is serious — serious enough to threaten our collective safety. Honestly, if Lorelai wasn't in the family way, I might not have broken down and begged your assistance like an utter weakling, but...

Madeleine smiled as she read, knowing Jolene was anything but a weakling. She was one of the strongest people she'd ever met. It was still a shock, though, to absorb the fact that her two friends were serving as detectives. Actual detectives! Even more shocking was the fact that they'd been keeping it from her.

The rest of Jolene's letter was an entreaty for Madeleine to trust Agent Evans and to allow him to explain the rest of what was going on.

One way or the other, I will see you soon. I promise! However, I am currently working undercover, which is why it is difficult for me to travel to Midland Hills right now. I am also reluctant to let Lorelai out of my sight, even for a few hours...

That didn't sound good! Madeleine quickly finished the rest of the letter, swallowing the emotion that rose to her throat at the possibility that Lorelai and her unborn child might be in danger. From whom or what, she had no earthly idea, but she was about to find out.

She folded the letter and met Garen Evans' inquiring look. "I'm ready to hear whatever it is you have to say, sir." Pressing a hand to her heart, she willed the heavy pounding to settle back to a more normal cadence. Her stomach felt like it was twisted into a dozen knots.

He glanced furtively around them and reached for her travel bag. "Follow me."

They strolled down the side of the clay-packed street. An occasional gust of wind kicked up sand and tumbleweeds. Simple clapboard structures rose on both sides of them. She spied a bakery and a post office, then a telegraph office. It was Friday, so most of them were open for business. A few doors down from the telegraph office, Garen Evans ushered her up a set of wooden steps to a weathered porch.

"This is my office, ma'am. Though other agents travel here from time to time, I'm the only one who works here on a regular basis. No, that isn't entirely true. My secretary puts in nearly as many hours as I do. Just not today. She's out of the office tending to a sick grandchild."

Madeleine gave a cluck of sympathy. "I am sorry to hear it."

"You and me both, Miss Caruthers. I'm a bit lost without her — certainly a lot less organized. Oh, and the coffee is colder when she's not around."

A chuckle escaped Madeleine. His honesty was so delightful that it quelled some of the butterflies flitting inside her belly. "I hope her grandchild recovers in record time."

"Lord willing." He threw open the front door to his office. Waving a hand, he ushered her inside.

She stepped past him and was surprised to hear him slide the bolt in place behind them.

When she glanced over her shoulder, he gave her an apologetic look. "Though it may seem like overkill at first, you will soon understand our need for such high security measures. This office is unmarked for good reason. The locals think we're a future government land and title office, undergoing an indefinite number of renovations before we open. Since there's an actual land and title office a few streets away, we don't get much attention. We haul a few boards in and out of here and swing hammers a few times per day to keep up the ruse. If anyone gets overly curious about what's going on, we'll simply relocate elsewhere."

Madeleine glanced around the near-empty room and was amazed to see the evidence of what he'd described. The front windows were boarded up, and individual planks of varying sizes leaned against the walls. A few hammers were scattered across the floor.

Agent Evans set her bag down near the door. "My office is in the back." He beckoned her to follow him.

"What we mostly do here," he explained as they walked, "is train new recruits. We additionally compile reports for the home office on the status of our ongoing cases in the area."

"Jolene indicated in her letter to me that you are well-versed on the case my friends are currently working on," she mused, wondering if he'd be willing to shed more light on the situation.

"I am, Miss Caruthers, and I'm about to tell you all about it. Please. Come in and have a seat." He unlocked and opened yet another door.

On the other side was a tastefully decorated office. Unlike the rest of the building, it was clean and orderly. A heavy wooden desk that was piled with papers dominated the room. A crystal paperweight in the shape of a cowboy boot rested on one of the stacks.

Garen Evans moved behind the desk to light a single lantern. Madeleine stepped forward to claim one of the two high-back chairs on the other side of the desk. Only when she was seated did he sit.

"It's a cattle rustling case," he announced with no more preamble. He clasped his hands on his desk and leaned his tall frame forward to look her straight in the eye. "We believe it's run by a man who calls himself Malvado."

It meant evil. She let out a huff of air. "That's a rather ominous name."

He nodded in approval. "I see that you know a little Spanish."

"Only a little." She frowned. "What's his real name?"

"According to an informant, whom we have every reason to believe is reliable, his name is Oliver Dugal."

"And this informant is?"

"His half-brother, Antonio Dugal."

She folded her arms, fascinated by what she'd learned so far. "Why would you believe the brother of the accused to be a reliable source for anything?"

Garen Evans' lips twitched. "You are exactly how your friends described you, and I couldn't be happier about that fact."

She raised her eyebrows at him.

He spread his hands. "Methodical and logical. You've never been trained as an agent, but already you know what questions to ask. You already have the mindset of a detective, Miss Caruthers."

She chuckled. "A very clever recruitment speech disguised as a compliment. I like it."

His grin widened. "Nothing gets past you, does it?"

She unfolded her arms and sat forward in her seat. "It's both a blessing and a curse, believe me, Agent Evans."

He wrinkled his forehead at her. "I know we've only just met, but would it be too much trouble to ask you to call me Garen? I'm already close friends with the husbands of your two best friends and, well..." He let his words settle in the air between them.

"And now you're playing the familiar card. You're very good at this recruitment stuff, Garen."

"Indeed I am, Madeleine. May I call you Madeleine?"

She sniffed. "My gut says that telling my future boss no won't earn me any points."

He guffawed. "In case no one has ever told you this, you're a real treat to converse with."

She made a face at him. "What if I told you no? What if I said I have no interest in becoming a detective? What would happen if I walked out of your office right now? I reckon my body would never be found, eh?"

"You're not going to tell me no." He made a scoffing sound, which she could only hope was a denial of what she'd suggested. "You're sitting forward in your chair, eagerly gobbling up every word about your friends and the case they're working. Your eyes are flashing with interest and intelligence."

More like desperation, mister. She wasn't in a position of strength in their conversation. They both knew it.

"Ah. More compliments. I like compliments." She deliberately settled back in her seat, hating to admit he was right. It was true, though. She was enjoying herself more than she had in a long time. "And if I agree to such a preposterous proposal, what would the next few days of my life look like?"

An admiring gleam brightened in his gaze. He picked up the crystal paperweight and tossed it in the air. It looked like a celebratory move from her perspective.

Catching it, his gaze sobered. "I will have you sign a contract of employment and advance some funds from your first month's salary. That way, you can purchase a few much-needed supplies. Either this afternoon or in the morning, we will visit a dressmaker and have a few gowns made for you. I will additionally offer you accommodations in the loft apartment above our heads for the next several days, or I will put you up at the nearest inn, whichever you prefer. There's a new one down the road that opened for business a mere week ago. The cost of your living arrangements will be covered by my office budget. Two days from now, you'll stand before a licensed minister and exchange vows with one of our most seasoned agents in a marriage of convenience. You will train with him. And when you are ready, you will work undercover with him to assist in the aforementioned cattle rustling case."

"A marriage of convenience, eh?" Madeleine's eyes felt like they were popping out of her head. She wasn't entirely sure what the convenience part meant, not that it really mattered. Her only regret was the fact she would *not* be marrying the man of her dreams. Pastor Josh Michaelson's face floated through her mind, the same way it had in every single one of her daydreams for the past year — silly, frivolous daydreams about love and happily-ever-after. Sadly, those were things that a working girl wasn't likely to enjoy. Not now. Not ever. So, if this marriage of convenience nonsense Agent Evans was spouting about involved a paying job, she couldn't afford to pass it up.

"Yes, a marriage of convenience," he confirmed in a matter-of-fact voice.

Good gracious! The man certainly wasn't very forthcoming with the details. She realized she was going to have to take a more direct approach. "Which is what, exactly?" she pressed.

"Whatever you want it to be." He fixed her with a bland look. "That's the convenient part. It can be anything from a strictly professional relationship to a real marriage. It's entirely up to you and him."

A professional relationship it is. Gulping away the last of her silly, girlish dreams, Madeleine nodded resolutely. "Why are you speaking in the present tense?" It was as if he was assuming she'd already made up her mind.

"Because, as I previously stated, you're not going to turn me down."

"You know this for a fact?" she taunted. *But only because I cannot afford not to, you mercenary cad!*

"I do." He tossed the paperweight into the air and caught it again. "What other questions do you have for me, Madeleine?"

"Why a marriage of convenience?" She wrinkled her nose, not entirely sure it was necessary. "Why not simply pose as a married couple? Why make it official?"

"A fair question that deserves a fair answer." He pursed his lips. "For one thing, posing as a married couple often requires sharing lodging accommodations. If you slept in separate rooms, you'd fool nobody into believing you were well and truly wed."

"Who cares if we're working undercover?"

"You'll be working undercover here in Bull County," he reminded. "Among folks you know, which means your reputation would be sorely compromised if you did not wed."

"Is it common practice to marry off your junior female agents like this?" She tried, but failed, to hide the sarcastic tone of her voice. It sounded almost barbaric to her, like those arranged marriages of old.

"Only when the case necessitates it." He tossed the crystal boot in the air again. "If you and your groom are not compatible, you may annul your union with the full blessing of the Pinkerton Agency before you move on to your next assignment. Assuming, that is, you've not yet consummated your relationship."

"Not yet—?" *Oh, dear!* Blushing madly, she blew out a whoosh of air. It felt scandalous to even discuss such matters, but what did she know? According to Fannie Miller, Madeleine was an old spinster relic, who didn't know the first thing about how to attract a man's attention. She'd danced a few times at town picnics and such, but she'd never officially courted anyone.

A fascinating thought struck her. "Is that how Lorelai and Jolene met their husbands?"

"Indeed, it is."

"I see," she said faintly, beginning to feel as if too much was happening too quickly. She needed a moment to catch her breath.

To her relief, Garen Evans let a comfortable silence settle between them.

"So, this marriage of convenience isn't optional?" she inquired at last. "If I accept the case, I must follow through with the marriage, as well."

"That is correct, but not to worry. You'll soon discover how useful it is to work undercover as a married woman. It's so much easier to blend into whatever environment you find yourself in. A man who drifts in town alone on assignment arouses immediate suspicion." He waved his hands in the air. "Folks want to know who he is, why he's here, and what he wants. An unattached woman would find herself even more limited in terms of where she can go and what she can accomplish without a proper chaperone. A happily married couple, on the other hand, is swiftly invited to teas, luncheons, and parties. Doors open to them that would not otherwise be open to agents who remain unwed."

Madeleine nodded ruefully, unable to deny any of his claims. It left her with only one more question. "Do you know the name of the agent I will wed two days from now?"

"Of course." He returned the paperweight to his desk and faced her again. "Here comes the trickiest part of our discussion."

"Why is that?" Her heart started to hammer again.

"There's a chance that you've already made the fellow's acquaintance."

How is that possible? "But I've only just arrived into town." Her breathing turned shallow as her mind raced blindly over the possibilities. She was acquainted with quite a few gentlemen back in Missouri, but none here in Texas.

"He's from Missouri, Madeline." He watched her closely. "The same town you hail from."

"Oh." Her power of speech seemed to be suddenly reduced to a single syllable. It was difficult to breathe as she waited for Garen to elaborate.

"He's a pastor at one of the churches there."

So great was her agitation at this latest revelation that she leaped to her feet and started pacing the small office.

"Is this going to be a problem, Madeleine?"

She pressed her hands to her bosom, mentally replaying her last encounter with Pastor Josh Michaelson. *Please don't go,* he'd said. *It's a dangerous place.* He'd known so much about the town where she was heading, and he'd asked some very pointed questions about her friends, such as what their husbands did for a living.

She halted her pacing. "It's only going to be a problem if his name is Josh Michaelson." Her voice shook a little.

Agent Evans scowled in contemplation. "Ah. You *do* know him."

"Yes." She glanced away, gulping at the discovery that the handsome and eloquent man of her dreams had turned out to be a Pinkerton agent. She truly hadn't seen this coming. Did it mean he wasn't really a pastor? *Mercy, but this undercover stuff is confusing!*

"How well do you know him, Madeleine?"

She blinked at the question. "Not very well, I suppose. He was my pastor."

"How is that a problem?"

"Oh, for pity's sake!" She rounded in agitation on him. "For a seasoned agent, you're a little slow on the uptake."

"Am I?" His expression relaxed into amused lines. "I take it your feelings are engaged?"

"Exactly," she snapped. "A fact he must never find out."

"You're right." His voice was dry. "For the life of

me, I cannot fathom anything worse than marrying a man you're already fond of."

She glared at his sarcasm. "I said my feelings are engaged, Garen. His are not."

His upper lip curled as he surveyed her more closely. "When was the last time you looked into a mirror, Miss Caruthers?"

For a moment, her glare deepened. Women of her financial circumstances generally could not afford the luxury of owning mirrors, for pity's sake! Then the truth sank in. The agent sitting in front of her was handing her yet another compliment. The kindness and barely concealed amusement in his expression indicated that he did not find her appearance to be abhorrent.

She sniffed in disdain. "There's really no need to keep buttering me up, since you've already guessed the truth. I'm going to accept your offer."

"Excellent!" He clapped his hands.

She gritted her teeth, wishing his triumph wasn't so obvious. Even if she could've afforded a return ticket to Missouri, she would've faced a life of endless drudgery there. Whereas in the short time she'd been conversing with Garen, he'd painted a picture of her taking control of her destiny, earning a decent living, and experiencing adventures she'd only dreamed about before now.

Then there was the matter of the promise she'd made to her friends years ago. That alone would have kept her in

Bull County for the time being. If only Josh Michaelson hadn't been dragged into the equation, the opportunity would have been perfect. Most unfortunately, her attraction to him was very real. It had been difficult enough to hide her feelings from him while she was a member of his congregation. She had no idea how she was going to continue hiding them after they were wed.

"I'm sorry to be the cause of any discomfort." The lead detective's lips twitched as he shuffled a few papers around on his desk. Leaning forward, he uncapped his inkwell.

"You don't look very sorry to me," Madeleine observed wryly. "You resemble a cat caught with cream all over his whiskers."

He guffawed and wrote something on the paper in front of him. "I don't know whether I should be pleased or alarmed that you find my thoughts to be so transparent."

She hastily changed the subject. "I'll gladly accept your offer to stay in the loft quarters overhead." She saw no point in draining his budget with the added expense of a boarding house room.

He inclined his head in agreement. "A wise choice, considering you'll have the whole floor to yourself. It has a small kitchen that my secretary restocked a few days ago. Plus, there's a powder room with a bathtub and running water."

She stared at him in amazement, wondering if she'd heard right. Then she pinched her arm for good measure.

"I assure you that you're awake, Madeleine."

She wrinkled her nose at him. "You weren't supposed to see that."

He chuckled and slid the paper he'd been writing on in her direction. "If you'll sign here and here," he pointed at the two spots on the form, "I'll process your application today, new recruit."

Chapter 4: Undercover Marriage

JOSH

Two days later

JOSH STRODE off the train in Midland Hills and took the stairs two at a time. He was carrying a travel bag in each hand. It was a good feeling to have his shoes planted firmly back on the ground. Though he enjoyed traveling, a man could easily get his fill of it after a full week or more on a train. Plus, he was more than ready to tackle his next case.

No one was at the platform to greet him, and he hadn't expected them to be. A hasty telegram received at one train stop had resulted in an answering telegram from him at the next stop, and so on and so forth. That was how he and Garen Evans had communicated throughout his journey west. They often wrote in code to each other, using pre-agreed-upon euphemisms, instead of the actual points they were discussing. When it came to transmitting numbers and addresses, they employed simple cyphers that changed depending on the day of the week — yet another precaution they employed.

Because of the telegram Josh had received yesterday, he knew he was supposed to meet with the lead detective on his next case at an unmarked building a few doors down from the telegraph office. He also knew he was supposed to first check in at the brand new Broken Wheel Inn, change into a construction uniform that had been deposited for him there prior to his arrival, and show up for duty with a toolbox in hand. Lastly, he understood that he would be exchanging vows with a new female recruit in a marriage of convenience.

If he was being honest with himself, getting married was the only part of the case he wasn't looking forward to. That, and the fact that Garen had been a little cagey with the details about his forthcoming nuptials. For one thing, he'd utterly omitted sharing the name of Josh's bride-to-be.

Lord, please let it be Madeleine Caruthers. Josh had puzzled through the details of his new assignment from every angle, and he kept coming to the same conclusion. It was more than just wishful thinking on his part, too. Sheer logic told him it was a very viable possibility he'd be wed to Madeleine before nightfall.

He was a man of deep and tremendous faith, which meant he got to believe in things like divine guidance, answered prayers, and miracles. And it would be just like the great and mighty God he preached about every

Sunday to provide him with another opportunity to court Madeleine. He knew this because he believed, without any reservations, that he served the God of second chances.

For this reason, it was with a skip in his step and a whistle on his lips that he made his way toward Garen Evans' office with his toolbox in hand. He didn't want to even consider the possibility that he would soon be married to someone other than Madeleine.

And if he was fortunate enough to enjoy a second chance with the woman of his dreams, Josh planned to do everything in his power not to botch things up between them again. Though he wasn't overly enamored with her decision to become a Pinkerton agent, he *was* enamored with the thought of being married to her the day she took on such risk. Assuming she couldn't be talked out of it, he very much preferred to be the agent who'd be training and protecting her.

Whistling a little louder, he arrived at the porch of Agent Evans' unmarked office. He gave a few test swings of his hammer against one of the porch columns to announce his arrival. Then he worked his way around the building, noisily lifting and moving several loose boards in the process. Eventually, he made it all the way to the back entrance.

The door opened, and he stepped inside.

A tall man with humor glinting in his eyes appeared in the dim hallway and held out a hand. "There you are!"

Josh clasped it firmly. "Hello to you, too." He was

half-tempted to sock his friend in the gut for his high-handedness in arranging a marriage of convenience on his behalf.

"The minister and your bride-to-be are waiting in my office." Garen waved a hand at the closed door on the other side of the room. "Do you have any final questions before we go inside to greet them?"

"Just please assure me that Madeleine Caruthers is the new recruit waiting for me on the other side of that door." He couldn't bear the thought of marrying anyone else, even temporarily.

Garen's eyebrows shot heavenward. "She is. How did you know?"

"Why do you ask?" Josh doubted his friend's reasons had anything to do with the case.

"Curiosity."

Josh snorted. "I rarely satisfy curiosity. You know that."

"Fine." Garen nodded, eyes twinkling. "As a friend, I'll leave it at this. I hope the agency's choice of partners is not going to be a problem for you."

Josh spread his hands. "Do I look like an unhappy man to you?"

Garen gave him a curious, searching look. "Madeleine claims you already known each other."

"Now you're fishing." Josh moved around him to cross the room to his friend's office.

"I enjoy fishing." Garen sounded like he was trying not to laugh as he followed. "You could at least throw me a worm, Agent Michaelson. One small, wiggly little worm is all I'm asking for."

"You're right. I could, but I won't." Certainly not before he laid eyes on Madeleine and figured out how she was taking the whole marriage of convenience twist in their collective fate.

Josh twisted the door handle and stepped inside the office.

Madeleine, who was pacing the small area, whirled at the sound to face him.

He'd rehearsed their encounter dozens of times before he entered the room, but there was no way he could've prepared himself for the astounding changes in her appearance. She was beautiful the last time he'd seen her — and every other time he'd seen her, for that matter. She was utterly enchanting now.

Her shabby gown had been replaced with a new gown, one of navy fabric with ivory lace trim at the neckline and wrists. Her boots and gloves were new, as well. Even the expression in her clear, assessing blue gaze had undergone a complete metamorphosis. It was both more confident and more shuttered than he remembered. Only her loose up-do of white-blonde hair remained the same as that of the woman who'd departed his church congregation a week ago. The waves were forever escaping the pins holding them in place, making him yearn to reach out and smooth back the stray strands.

He paused right inside the doorway. "Thank you

for agreeing to marry me, Miss Caruthers." He saw no point in beating around the bush.

There was a gentleman, whom he did not recognize, seated in an upholstered chair in front of Garen's desk. Josh spared the fellow no more than a cursory glance, presuming it was the minister who would marry them. He was too busy drinking in the sight of Madeleine.

Her cheeks turned a bright shade of pink at his words, though her expression did not change. "You do not look surprised, sir."

"Neither do you."

She attempted to tuck a strand of silky hair behind one ear. It promptly swung back to dangle against her cheek. "It wasn't hard to connect the dots after my arrival, considering the strangeness of our last encounter."

"Strangeness!" He muffled a chuckle, feeling rueful. *Good gravy!* He'd spent the last week reliving the magic of every second they'd shared between them, every word, every touch.

She waved a hand, emitting a breathy chuckle. "Some of the questions you asked me made no sense at the time. The vocations of my friends' husbands, for one thing."

"I see." He'd not given any thought to how she would view such questions. He'd been too shocked to discover where she was traveling, too anxious to discover the extent of her friends' involvement in his current assignment. Not that he minded her connecting the dots. She was someone he trusted implicitly. If she'd been anyone else, he'd have probably chosen his questions more carefully, so as not to arouse such curiosity.

Garen, who'd been standing on the threshold watching their exchange, shut the door and moved across the office to stand behind his desk. "Agent Michaelson, your bride-to-be has shown a particular affinity for reading thoughts, expressions, and motivations. Anything you wish to hide from her, you'd best hide it carefully."

Josh wanted to roll his eyes at his friend's ill-concealed attempt to take a humorous jab at his feelings for Madeleine. His only comfort was that she had no idea what the man was talking about.

Or so he hoped.

His gaze returned to his future wife and partner, catching her beautiful gaze and plundering it for answers.

Her lips parted, and she drew in a sharp breath. Then she glanced away from him. Facing Garen, she announced, "I am ready to move forward with our agreement and become an agent." Her soft, controlled voice didn't fool Josh one bit. The way her fingers twisted in her skirt as she spoke told him she was as apprehensive about their forthcoming nuptials as he was, and she had every right to be.

After spending an entire year in his congregation, he'd not once made any moves to court her. In hindsight, his actions were paltry, surly, and downright unfair to her. He should've complimented her appearance or gifted her with flowers. He should've escorted her to a church picnic while he had the chance. He'd been an utter fool to avoid enjoying her company. He should have done so at every opportunity.

Instead, he'd allowed her to leave town alone and travel straight into the jaws of danger. Though she appeared well, he inwardly shuddered at the thought of the harm that might've befallen her while journeying without a chaperone.

As a result, he was about to marry a woman who had no idea how strong or how deeply his feelings for her ran. There would be no more escaping them.

Squaring his shoulders, he followed her announcement with one of his own. "Be assured, I am equally ready to assist Miss Caruthers in her training and development." Setting his toolbox down on the floor, he stepped forward to take his place at her side.

The minister rose from his chair, looking mildly bored with the goings-on in the room. He was a pale, slender creature with a receding hairline and jagged fingernails that looked as if he occasionally nibbled on them. To make matters worse, his plain black suit looked more appropriate for a funeral than a wedding. Josh wondered where Garen had scrounged up such a dismal-looking fellow.

While the man fiddled with his Bible and the notes he'd stashed inside it, Josh leaned closer to Madeleine. "I'm grateful for your safe arrival in Bull County," he informed her quietly. "I prayed for you every day since your departure."

She grew very still at his words. There was a long pause before she responded. "Thank you, sir."

Though she spoke in a voice barely above a whisper, Garen must have overheard her. "I recommend you dispense with the formalities of titles and surnames, since you're getting married." He shot Josh a sly, knowing look that made Josh want to pop him in the nose for the mirth he was enjoying at their expense. "It might raise a few eyebrows around town to hear you referring to each other as ma'am and sir."

Madeleine gave a faint titter as she nodded. "That makes perfect sense."

"Shall we begin?" the minister interrupted in a nasally voice.

"Yes." Josh muffled a snort of derision. He was accustomed to beginning the wedding ceremonies he presided over with much more eloquent phrases, such as, "Dearly beloved, we are gathered here today in the House of God..." Unfortunately, they weren't standing inside a church. They were in a small office inside a building with boarded-up windows, standing before a man who looked like he would've been more comfortable in a funeral parlor.

The ceremony did not improve as it progressed. Josh was appalled at the way the minister stumbled over his words and even appeared to be close to yawning at one point. Josh had to grit his teeth to get through his vows without yanking the Bible from the fellow's hands and taking over the rest of the ceremony himself.

He was nothing short of relieved when it was over. He and Madeleine signed their marriage certificate and a few other forms, which the pale minister signed as their officiator. Garen then signed everything as their witness.

Only when the lead detective tried to hand Madeleine a ring commissioned by the agency did Josh recall the one he'd brought along with him. It had belonged to his mother. May she rest in peace. Somehow, the mood of the occasion didn't seem appropriate to bring up the existence of a family heirloom, so he resisted the urge to fish it from his pocket. He would give it to his bride later.

Instead, he watched as she mechanically slid the agency ring on her own finger. With a flickering glance in his direction, she silently exited the room to go upstairs and finish packing.

Josh waited until their horrendous excuse for a minister left the building before exploding, "Where on earth did you find such a despicable creature?"

"On the agency's list of approved ministers," Garen returned mildly. He was still seated behind his desk, filling out yet more forms. No doubt they were part of Madeleine's file as a new agent.

"He looks like he handles cadavers more often than live subjects."

"He might. I didn't ask." Garen continued to write.

"It seems to me you should care a smidgeon more about the caliber of people you employ to unite your agents in holy matrimony." Josh was aghast at his friend's cavalier attitude. Marriage was a sacred agreement and should be treated as such — forever and always.

Frowning, Garen finally laid down his pen and folded his hands. "Due to our line of business, my biggest concern is securing licensed officiators who will neither ask questions about the agency nor tell tales concerning their service to us after leaving my office. Sometimes that means we get to work with a dignified man-of-the-cloth. Other times, we get saddled with anomalies like Mr. Casket. I am sorry that was the case today, my friend."

Josh gave a grudging nod to accept his apology. However, he was saved from responding by Madeleine's reappearance. This time, she was garbed the same way he was — in work clothes with artfully placed smudges on her cheeks and chin.

"My bag is packed and waiting by the front door." She lifted her chin at Josh, as if bracing herself for what came next.

Both Josh and Garen stared back at her in amusement.

"Well, it's official," Josh drawled, as enchanted with her latest costume as he'd been with the gown she'd wed him in. "You are the most stunning woman I've ever met, no matter what you're wearing."

Her lips parted in surprise. "I do believe that's the

loveliest thing you've ever said to me, pastor...er, Josh."
Her attempt at sounding lighthearted was eclipsed by
the tremor in her voice.

Garen leaned back in his chair, crossing his arms.
"Do we need to hold an official training session on
how to address each other with familiarity before you
leave the building?"

Josh and Madeleine whipped their heads in his
direction and responded in unison. "No!"

He raised his hands in defense. "In that case, my
dear agents, I look forward to seeing you back here
bright and early in the morning. I know it's the weekend, but there's no time to waste. Your assistance is
urgently needed in our current case."

"When is bright and early?" Madeleine inquired
faintly.

"First light." Though Garen stood in dismissal, his
eyes twinkled knowingly at his friend. Josh could feel
his mirth long after he and his bride exited the
building.

JOSH AND MADELEINE tromped in silence
to the Broken Wheel Inn. Only after they were
ensconced inside his quarters did he speak. "Well, that
was about as far from the marriage ceremony I envi-
sioned as we could get." He set her travel bag on the
edge of the four-poster bed. It was covered in a red,
white, and blue patchwork quilt.

The inn wouldn't qualify as posh, but it was filled with rustic, homey furniture. Most importantly, it was clean. There was a stacked stone fireplace across from the bed, a small writing desk against one wall, and a buttery yellow ceramic washbasin on a table beside it. A trio of iron hooks provided ample space for hanging clothing. Last but not least, a white crocheted valance framed the only window in the room.

Since they were staying on the second floor, it gave them a decent view of the street below them.

Madeleine gave a nervous titter at his words. "The minister was rather ghastly, was he not?"

Josh's upper lip curled. "In an otherworldly sort of way, yes." He turned impulsively to his new bride. "We should get married again, Madeleine."

Her lovely blue eyes widened. "After our case is closed?" A soft, vulnerable light crept into them.

"I'd rather do it now."

"Indeed," she squeaked.

He sought to explain himself. "Since we're married, I'd like to actually *feel* married."

"Mmm..." He wasn't certain by the sound she emitted if she was agreeing or disagreeing with him.

Rummaging in the drawer of the small cabinet beside the bed, he removed his Bible.

"Oh, you mean *right now!*"

"I do." He walked back around the bed to stand before her. Opening his Bible, he muttered, "Some might call me a fool for doing this, but I married one of the most incredible women I've ever known. From my very own congregation, no less. You deserve better than what you had to endure back in Garen Evans' office."

"I hardly know what to say about this new version of you." Madeleine waved her hands helplessly at him.

He frowned at her words. "What do you mean?"

"In the past, you were content to be married to your job. Please know that I am more than capable of doing the same." She tossed her head. "There's no need to fret about my sensibilities concerning what has transpired between us."

Her words brought to mind a boxer retreating to his corner of the ring. "I *was* married to my job," he confessed, hating the necessity of keeping her at arm's length in the past. "Some might argue that I still am, considering that our marriage was a job requirement."

Though Madeleine's chin remained high, her shoulders slumped. It made him realize he'd botched yet another chance to woo her properly.

"Eh, hang it all!" he sighed. Coming clean with his new bride was more difficult than he'd ever imagined it would be.

"Pastor, er, Josh!" She gave a delicate cough, struggling to school her expression. "I am not accustomed to hearing such strong language from you."

"You're not accustomed to me acting like a regular fellow in any fashion," he retorted drearily. "It is my fault entirely, since I've been playing a role the entire time we've known each other."

"Wh-what do you mean?" She shifted her weight from one foot to the other.

"As an undercover agent, I was forced to maintain the strictest levels of professionalism at all times." He shook his head. "Even though I longed to be friendlier with you."

She caught her lower lip between her teeth, but she didn't say anything. The gesture emboldened him to continue. "I swore an oath to protect the integrity of my office, the cases I work, and everyone involved in them." Surely she understood now that she'd taken the same oath herself.

Wishing she'd say something, he thumbed through the pages of his Bible until he found the passage he was looking for. "The first time I ever let my guard down around you was the day you informed me you were leaving town."

Madeleine grew pale and started fiddling with one of the buttons on the sleeve of her dingy work dress.

He rushed to fill the silence. "Allow me to right one of the wrongs between us by giving you a proper wedding ceremony. One that is closer to what you deserve, at least."

"Very well, Josh." Her voice was thready. The light in her eyes had turned vulnerable.

Her willingness to give him another chance spread warmly through his chest, encouraging him to continue what he'd started. He lifted his Bible and started to speak. "Dearly beloved, let us be united in holy matrimony all over again, this time by a man of

God who firmly believes in the sanctity of marriage." He spoke directly to her, utterly entranced when her lips parted in surprise and her breathing seemed to turn shallow.

He read one of his favorite verses about love from I Corinthians. "Love is patient, love is kind. It does not envy, it does not boast, it is not proud." He raised his gaze once again to Madeleine. Then he recited the rest of the verse from memory, not wanting to miss one nuance of the expressions churning across her delicate features — cautious hope warring with a carefully concealed longing that he shared with every ounce of his being.

"It is not rude," he continued quietly. "It is not self-seeking, it is not easily angered, it keeps no record of wrongs. Love does not delight in evil but rejoices in the truth. It always protects, always trusts, always hopes, always perseveres. Love never fails."

He closed his Bible. "And that, my dear Madeleine, is the verse that I think you most embody. Never have I met a more patient and kind human being. You are the least boastful, least proud, least self-seeking person I've ever known. I've watched you trust, hope, and persevere against some of the most difficult odds while serving as a member of my congregation. I watched you work your fingers to the bone to make ends meet, and still you found time to lend a hand to those less fortunate than you. I cannot recall how many times I looked across my congregation and inwardly declared what a perfect pastor's wife you would make, if only I'd been free to pursue you."

He set his Bible on the bed and turned to take her hands in his. "It may be a little late to declare such things to you, but it doesn't make them any less true."

She blinked back tears. "I don't know what to say, Josh." Her lips trembled as she spoke.

"How about we recite our vows again to each other?"

A lone tear streaked down her cheek as she nodded.

In that moment, he realized he'd peeled back the layers to reveal her most vulnerable, breakable self. *Lord, give me the strength to do things right this time around.*

"I'll start us off," he assured gently. "I, Josh Michaelson."

"I, Madeleine Caruthers." Her voice shook a little.

"Do take thee as my wedded wife."

"Do take thee as my wedded husband."

He gazed longingly into her eyes as they spoke the age-old promises to each other. "According to God's holy ordinance," he concluded with utmost reverence. "Amen and amen."

"Amen," she echoed breathlessly.

"May I kiss you, Madeleine?"

Her color heightened and her slender fingers tightened on his, but she did not pull back as his head descended over hers.

His mouth brushed the curve of her lips as lightly

as the first blanket of winter snow, yet warmer. Much warmer. He did not deepen the kiss. It was too soon for such intimacies. Now was the time for sweetness and tenderness. The time to honor and cherish.

The way her lips trembled against his moved him deeply. He reveled in the blind trust she'd always given him, even when he'd not done a single thing to deserve it.

This time will be different. He silently vowed again to treasure and revere her as the precious gift that she was. *Until the end of my days, so help me.*

He lifted his head. "I feel married to you now." It was a feeling that inspired both awe and humbleness. It was a feeling that additionally made him want to drop to a knee in front of her — to thank her for honoring him with her hand in marriage.

Her eyelids slowly opened, revealing luminous blue eyes swimming with emotions that reached deep inside his heart and found a home there. "I feel married to you, too, Josh."

He reached into his pocket to withdraw his mother's wedding ring. "This is the ring I want you to wear. It belonged to my mother. May I replace your agency ring with it?"

"But of course!" She held out her hand to him and watched in silence as he removed her agency ring and slid the Michaelson one in its place. "It's so beautiful," she breathed, turning her hand so the emerald caught the light and flashed blue-green fire up at them.

"I couldn't agree more." His tone was so fervent that her startled gaze darted back to his.

Whatever she saw in his expression made her blush — deeply. Her voice was light, however, when she started speaking again. "Thank you for exchanging vows with me again. If only we weren't wearing the grungiest outfits in all of Texas," she sighed mournfully.

He snickered down at her mud-colored gown, wanting nothing more than to swoop in for another kiss. Instead, he settled for brushing his thumb against one of the smudges on her cheek. "My dearest Mrs. Michaelson, would you allow me the honor of escorting you downstairs to the dining room?"

"In this dress?" She sounded aghast.

"Unfortunately, yes. Not only is it part of our new role, I am famished enough not to care as much as I otherwise would. What do you say, madam?" He took a step away back and held out his hand to her.

As if on cue, her stomach growled. With a self-conscious chuckle, she clapped one slender hand over the noisy organ. "Since you're such a seasoned detective, Agent Michaelson, I'll leave you to interpret that response for yourself."

"It's telling, indeed." It was one of the happiest moments in his life when she placed her hand in his. Then they strolled together to the dining room.

Chapter 5: First Assignment

MADELEINE

MADELEINE TREASURED every moment of her first evening with Josh. Over the next several days, she found herself clinging to her memory of that evening like a lifetime. There were even moments when she wondered if she'd imagined their idyllic second exchange of vows right before dinner. Because the very next morning, her groom commenced a truly punishing training regimen.

His handsome features were devoid of emotion as he dispassionately taught her how to sprint in a zig-zagging motion in order to avoid flying bullets. He also showed her how to low crawl her way across terrain so rugged that it left her scraped and bruised. Then there were entire afternoons of handling and shooting weapons — so many different ones that the details of how to load and unload each of them started to blur together.

"Again," her husband barked on the seventh

morning of her training. He dropped to his hands and knees to examine her slithering through the final few yards of a particularly daunting obstacle course. "After you clean your rifle, of course." He rose to his feet, dusting his hands. "During your next repetition through the course, be more careful with your weapon. A muzzle jammed with dirt isn't going to fire properly when you're facing a posse of bad *hombres*."

Gritting her teeth, Madeleine dragged her aching limbs upright and faced him. "Are you sure we're doing this right?" she grumbled. "I'm not going to live to face a single outlaw if you kill me in these blasted training exercises!"

"Why, Madeleine Michaelson!" He drew back dramatically, one hand pressed mockingly to his chest. "I don't believe I've ever heard you use such strong language."

It was such an accurate imitation of her accusation from a few days ago that she was tempted to laugh. However, she refused to give him the satisfaction. She was too frustrated by his callous treatment during their first week of training sessions. Instead, she glowered at him, trying not to admire his well-corded forearms that his rolled-up shirtsleeves had on such enticing display. He was as dusty and sweaty as she was in a pair of ripped and patched denim trousers.

In the end, her irritation won out over the humor he'd attempted to inject into their lesson.

"Is that what you're really trying to do?" she demanded, lurching across the yard to slam her weapon down on the trestle table where she'd loaded, unloaded, assembled, and disassembled it dozens of times already. "Kill me? Or discourage me, perhaps? You never wanted me to travel to Midland Hills in the first place, did you? Never wanted me to become an agent?" Her movements were jerky with exhaustion as she proceeded to clean the gunk from the muzzle of her weapon.

As much as it pained her to admit it, even to herself, she was progressing quickly beneath his harsh brand of training. In one short week, he'd taught her dozens of ways to defend herself. He'd also taught her the fundamentals of good old-fashioned detective work. Last but not least, his strict physical fitness regimen was already strengthening her body. Plus, he was right about the fact that her horrid weapon was not going to fire properly until she succeeded in clearing the debris from her muzzle.

"On the contrary, my dear," Josh's voice was coolly impersonal as he surveyed her work with his hands on his hips, "I'm trying to keep you alive." He pointed to a spot of dirt she'd missed. "Make sure you get it all, Agent Michaelson. One ill-placed clod of dirt can send a bullet off-course and change the outcome of a hostile encounter."

His dry commentary proved to be the last straw. Tossing her weapon aside, she advanced on him, seething.

"Is this what our marriage is going to be like going forward?" she ground out. "Nothing more than harsh words, scrapes, bruises, sweat, blood, and tears?"

He held his ground, glaring down at her as she moved to stand directly in front of him. "I'm doing my job, Madeleine. Everything in my power to develop your skills as an agent, thereby increasing your chances of success in the field."

"Your job, eh?" She jabbed a finger against his chest. "It's always about the job, isn't it? The same job that kept us apart for an entire year. The same job—"

"That brought us together," he reminded, slapping his hand over hers. His larger hand flattened hers against his heart.

They stood there, chests heaving and eyes snapping at each other.

"I can't help wondering," she rasped, "if the man who quoted 1 Corinthians 13:4 to me a week ago is still inside the barking, growling beast who's taken his place."

Josh's breath came out in a huff. It was as if she'd socked him in the gut with her fist. "He's still in there, Madeleine." His tone was low and tense, infused with warning.

Emboldened by his response, she pressed closer, tipping her face up to his. "Show me," she taunted. "Give me some proof that the Bible-toting pastor I married is still buried beneath all your snapping and snarling."

Though his gaze dropped to her lips, his jaw tight

ened stubbornly. "Madeleine, this isn't going to help us train."

"It's not going to help you continue to browbeat me, you mean?" She stood on her tiptoes, bringing their faces closer together.

"Eh, have it your way!" His arms came around her, and he covered her mouth with his.

With a sigh of exultation, she looped her hands around his neck and held on. This was what they'd been missing in their marriage. It was everything she'd been longing for.

The remaining resistance in him crumbled. The many months of keeping their distance from each other faded. Though his touch remained gentle, he drank her in like a man dying of thirst.

It was a long time before he lifted his head to nuzzle the corner of her mouth. "What have you done to me, Madeleine?"

"I hope that I've made you feel married again." She'd gotten more than she'd bargained for in the process, though she didn't regret it one bit. It thrilled her to discover that, beneath all of Josh Michaelson's blustering, was a man who longed for her the way she longed for him.

"I'm never going to stop feeling married to you," he assured huskily, cupping her face in his hands. "Not even during the hardest or hottest days of training."

The look he gave her elicited a delicious shiver. Lightly shoving at his chest to put distance between them, she reluctantly returned to cleaning her weapon.

"The next time you yell at me, I hope you remember how quickly you can be brought to heel with a single kiss."

He watched her with an inscrutable expression. "It wasn't something I ever doubted."

"You've sure had me doubting it." She vigorously rubbed every last vestige of dust and dirt from her rifle until the surface was clean enough to eat from. "In case you've forgotten, it wasn't a training regimen back in Missouri that earned you my initial trust and loyalty."

"Be that as it may, I've no desire to go back to the way we were before we traveled to Texas." His voice was tight as he moved to stand behind her. He peered over her shoulder to observe her progress with her weapon.

She closed her eyes against the rush of emotion his nearness brought.

He bent his head next to hers to speak quietly against her earlobe. "No matter how tough this training is on both of us, I don't want to go back to not being married to you, Madeleine."

His words resonated through her, shaking her in ways she'd never before been shaken. "Perhaps compromise is in order, then."

His hands came to rest on her waist as his mouth brushed the side of her neck. "What sort of compromise, Agent Michaelson?"

In that very moment, for no particular reason, key element of the case popped into her mind. "Josh! She spun around in his arms, knowing the timing wa horrible. However, the thought was too important to bury. They'd been discussing the case for days, mulling every possible direction the investigation could take.

"Yes, dearest?" He leaned in to nuzzle her temple.

She hated to shatter the intimacy of the moment with business, but every instinct in her was shouting that she was on to something with her latest theory. "How soon do you think Garen Evans could have our entire team assembled here in Midland Hills?"

"Is this the compromise we were discussing?" His expression was both quizzical and bemused.

"Not even close." She tugged his head down for a quick and tender peck on the lips. "I'd prefer we continue that particular conversation over a candlelit dinner," she paused to wag a finger at him, "after I've bathed off all ten inches of this miserable grime. And after I've had the opportunity to change into something that makes me resemble a female again."

"Then I very much look forward to dinner tonight." He winked at her. "Not that I find you anything less than captivating, britches and all." He bent to capture her mouth in a more lingering kiss than the one she'd just given him. "As for calling our team to Midland Hills, I can personally vouch for the fact that Garen has been champing at the bit to have such a meeting. I'm the one who's been holding off the dogs, so to speak. Insisting you need more time before throwing you fully into the fray as an agent."

Madeleine was greatly gratified to learn how much her husband had been protecting her, despite his gruff demeanor and despite all the tough training he'd put her through. "I'm ready, Josh."

"I know you are." He gave her a measuring look, one that was mixed with both pride and concern on her behalf. "I reckon we could pull off such a meeting in a matter of hours. Garen already has the entire team on standby. All they've been waiting for is..." He paused, giving her another searching look.

They've been waiting for me. And he'd been the one keeping them waiting until he was sure she was ready. Knowing that gave her the energy to step back from his embrace. Angling her head at the obstacle course she'd traversed earlier, she sighed, "I'm about to go throw myself back into that pile of rocks and tumbleweeds you so kindly arranged for today's training. While I suffer for the cause, let Garen know he can begin assembling the troops."

No small amount of admiration glinted in her husband's gaze as he watched her return to the training course.

"Oh, and be sure to include Antonio Dugal in our gathering, please." She glanced over her shoulder as she spun away from him. "Something tells me he will have a vital role to play in capturing his brother."

MOST UNFORTUNATELY, she had no opportunity to bathe or change before the arrival of their fellow agents.

Garen must have realized his office would never be big enough to hold them all, so he moved their huddle into the front room of the building. He and Josh dragged the three chairs from his office, then got to work assembling a few makeshift benches from the boards and blocks littering the room.

Jolene and Edgar Barella were the first to arrive. She glided like a queen through the back door ahead of her husband, took one look at Madeleine, and did a double take. She waited until the men had shut the door behind her, then she gave a muted war whoop and came hurtling in her direction.

"My lands, but you're a sight for sore eyes!" She hugged Madeleine tightly, then leaned back to take a look at her while gurgling with laughter. "Our sweet, demure, ladylike Madeleine." Still snickering, she reached down to give her friend's filthy trousers a tweak.

"You've got the sore part right. Ugh!" Madeleine flicked a clod of dirt off her shoulder and sent it scuttling across the room. "Steadfast tutor of small children, an expert laundress, and now the wife of the most ruthless detective in the state of Texas."

A round of snickers worked its way across the room at her words.

Jolene nearly doubled over with laughter. She flipped a handful of her dark hair over her shoulder as she shot a pointed look at her husband. "Like I told you, she's exactly what we needed!"

"That you did, minx." He expelled a long-suffering breath as he leaned around his wife to offer his hand to Madeleine. "Just for the record, this woman is forever giving me the how-to and the what-for. It's no wonder you drummed her out of Missouri on her ear. You'd have never gotten a moment of peace, otherwise."

Madeleine shook his hand, not missing the blast of unabashed adoration for Jolene in his aquamarine gaze, nor the way his fingers trailed possessively beneath her elbow as he taunted her.

They were in love. Madeleine had no doubt of it as she studied the unlikely pair. Edgar Barella was singularly unremarkable in his appearance. It was as if he'd purposely dressed to draw the least amount of notice to himself. His hair was streaked a dozen different shades of blonde from over-exposure to the sun. His rolled-up shirtsleeves displayed farmer tan lines at his wrists. His trousers were faded, and his boots were scuffed. In comparison, Jolene resembled the Queen of Sheba in an ostentatious red dress with real diamonds winking from her ears and throat.

Madeleine chuckled as she met Edgar's gaze. "Help me out here. You're working undercover as a handyman for Mrs. Brinkley's boarding house, while your bride is doing what, exactly?" She waved a hand helplessly at Jolene.

"Servicing as his deplorable trollop of a wife," her friend supplied. "A woman given to brazen and public displays of affection." She shot a cheeky smile at her husband, who waggled his eyebrows playfully in return. "His fault entirely. I'll let him do the explaining."

He winked at her. "Just for the record, I have no complaints about your undercover role — past, present, or otherwise." He moved in her direction with a wicked grin riding his features.

"You wouldn't!" She shot him a warning look. "In case you've forgotten, we are among friends, you cad."

He swooped in for a kiss, anyway. She dodged it. His mouth grazed her ear instead of its intended target.

Lorelai arrived in the midst of their shenanigans with her husband, John Langston, and her senior ranch hand, Antonio Dugal. She took one look at Madeleine and burst into happy tears. "I'm so glad you made it safely to Texas!" She rushed across the room to throw her arms around Madeleine. "I have missed you more than words can express."

Her belly was beginning to swell, causing the three women to pause and exclaim in delight over her coming jaunt into motherhood. Then Lorelai, who'd yet to finish hugging Madeleine, extended her other arm to Jolene. "Together again," she murmured into their huddle. "My heart is full. I couldn't possibly ask for more than this."

Her husband gently cleared his throat. "Well, love, as happy as I am about your reunion with your friends, I can and do ask for more." He was a portrait of polite reserve, the perfect match for the lovely Lorelai.

Madeleine caught his eye and nodded, instantly growing serious. "He's right. Our quest for justice is what brought us together today." She left the embrace of her friends to extend her hand to him. "It's a pleasure to finally meet you, Agent Langston. I've heard so much about you."

"John," he correctly quickly. "According to my wife, you're family."

She smiled her appreciation and held out her hand to Antonio Dugal next. "I have been looking forward to meeting you as well, sir."

"Likewise." He inclined his head graciously over her hand. He wore his auburn hair on the longish side, but his beard was short-clipped and tinged with frost. A Scottish gentleman to the bone, he proudly displayed a drape of green and blue plaid fabric over his left shoulder.

Madeleine's heart twisted at the thought of all the wrongs he'd endured. "I've read the reports about the cattle rustling case, Mr. Dugal, and let me just say this as the newest detective on our team. I want justice for you, your brother, his daughters, and for the woman you both loved and lost."

Pain lanced through his slate gray gaze. "I am no longer certain there's any justice to be had, ma'am." His words were bitter, but his tone was not. He was simply stating what he believed to be the facts.

"I can understand why you feel that way." Empathy squeezed her heart. "I've no plans to brow beat you into believing otherwise." Even justice couldn't restore all that had been taken from him.

"Thank you, ma'am." He inclined his head again, but there was gratitude mixed with the pain this time.

She'd managed to establish a bond with him. That was good. Pacing in front of him with her hands linked behind her back, she inwardly rehearsed what she, Garen, and Josh had prepared for today's meeting. As the newest recruit, she posed the smallest threat to Antonio, whom they were still trying to decide if they could trust, so Garen had instructed her to launch an interrogation that he wouldn't see coming — certainly not from her, of all people. They hoped to learn something from his initial reaction before he realized what they were up to.

"Those you lost cannot be returned to you," she mused in the same soft, kind voice, "at least not this side of glory. Pardon the religious reference, if that's not something you subscribe to." She gave a self-deprecatory chuckle. "As a minister's wife, it comes naturally to me."

Antonio sniffed. "I reckon the good Lord is about the only One who hasn't let me down at this point, lass."

Either he was a man of faith, or he was pretending to be one. Only further questioning could determine that.

She plunged back into the conversation. "I think everyone in the room would agree with that." She was pleased to see heads nodding. Garen hadn't been clear on whether or not he'd informed the other agents about their impromptu interrogation of Antonio.

"Not only have you suffered tremendous personal losses," Madeleine paused to give an exaggerated sigh, "it's the worst miscarriage of justice that you were subsequently accused of insanity." For claiming his half-brother, whom everyone else believed was dead, to be alive. She abruptly spun on her heels to face him. "What an uproar you created, Mr. Dugal, when you announced your brother is still alive." She sent him an admiring smile.

He shrugged. "I only spoke the truth."

She nodded excitedly. "Then you had the audacity to claim he's the mastermind behind the cattle rustlers we're tracking. If your testimony is ever proven to be correct, you'll literally turn dozens of deputy and marshal reports into lies."

He lifted his chin stubbornly. "Only because they are lies, lass!"

She could tell his ire was being stirred, which added authenticity to his responses.

Nodding vehemently, she declared, "I believe you, Mr. Dugal. I believe the reports are lies and that your brother still lives. What I don't understand, and I think what everyone in this room is trying to figure out, is why there are no less than seventeen official lawmen statements on record that claim otherwise."

He shrugged. "I think the evidence speaks for itself. Unfortunately, there are folks out there who don't want to hear the truth."

"The truth is that there are men wearing badges who purposely falsified their reports, right?" She studied him from beneath her lashes, wondering if he understood how preposterous that sounded.

He snorted with disdain. "That's my theory, but they won't believe you any more than they believed me, lass. So unless you want to end up in an insane asylum like I did..." He barked out a laugh that contained no mirth.

"Oh, it's more than a theory." She smiled innocently at him. "You know for a fact that those reports are false, because you know the man who pressured those poor lawmen into writing such hogwash."

A stunned expression settled across his features. It was chased by a shadow of guilt, then a shiver of remorse.

"What we need is a name, Mr. Dugal." She didn't want to give him too much time to think at this juncture. "You have a name in mind, don't you? Because you were serving in the Texas Police Force at the time, which — according to your own testimony — did nothing to help track down your family's murderer. More than likely because it was a prominent member of the police force who betrayed them. Maybe because they unwittingly witnessed something they weren't supposed to witness?" She'd considered long lists of possibilities, but that one seemed the most likely.

Antonio Dugal leaped up from the bench where he was sitting. "You have no idea what you're talking about, lass!"

"I wish I didn't, Mr. Dugal. I truly wish I didn't." However, she was the detective who'd been tasked with ripping the scabs from his wounds. None of the other agents in the room were taking any joy from watching it happen, but they understand that ranchers across the region were depending on their team to solve this case.

Real tears sprang to Madeleine's eyes as she warmed to the topic. "What brought me to this heart-breaking conclusion was the research I did on your sister-in-law. She wasn't loyal to anyone, was she, Mr. Dugal? Not to your brother, not to you, not even to the high-ranking official on the Texas Police Force, whom she was planning on running away with."

"Stop! Please stop!" He stomped across the room, dragging his hands through his hair.

"This was never about seeking justice for the woman you once loved, was it, Mr. Dugal? Because she crushed any feelings you ever had for her the day she broke your heart. This has always been about seeking justice for—"

"My daughter!" he shouted, throwing his hands toward the ceiling. "You're right. One of the young girls who perished was mine."

A shocked silence met his announcement. From the looks on the faces of her fellow agents, Madeleine deduced that most of them had not, in fact, been briefed about her role in today's interrogation.

In the ensuing hubbub, a tearful Mr. Dugal spilled the missing details of the case to them. What he had to say contained a few more surprises. For one thing, his brother, Oliver Dugal, wasn't truly a cattle rustler. The entire legend of Malvado had been fabricated to side-line the brothers' efforts to bring the real criminal mastermind to justice — a man by the name of Bando Brown, who was currently serving as a U.S. Marshal in Central Texas. Antonio's subsequent incarceration at the insane asylum had been part of Marshal Brown's efforts to stop the brothers.

"Every time we tried to cooperate with the authorities, there was an attempt made on our lives," Antonio concluded bitterly. "That's why we decided to take the law into our hands and bring Bando Brown to justice ourselves."

"I reckon that's also why you pretended to work with us," Lorelai concluded with a sigh of regret as she regarded one of her longest standing, most faithful employees. "You continued to propagate the legend of Malvado to gain access to our information and resources."

Antonio shrugged. "I didn't know what else to do. Three innocent girls were already in the ground, and my brother and I were dead men walking. We still are." He shook his head, looking grave.

"Maybe not," Garen cut in firmly. "I think we'd have a fighting chance at solving this case if you and Oliver would be willing to work with our team of detectives — for real this time."

Antonio plopped heavily back down on his bench. "Seems to me, all you really want is to stop the cattle rusting in your area. Oliver and I are the only ones trying to bring Bando Brown to justice."

In light of all the man's crimes, Madeleine doubted that Antonio considered a jail sentence to be fair. He likely wanted to see the man hang. Was his desire for revenge greater than his desire for justice?

"I don't see why we can't do both." Garen scowled at the Scotsmen, visibly affronted by the man's accusation.

Antonio spread his hands. "I've tried every method in the book and failed. I'm at a loss as to what we could try that hasn't already been tried."

"I can think of one thing." Garen grimaced as he glanced around the room. "No one is going to like my idea, though."

"You're right." Josh pushed away from the wall he'd been lounging against. "I've already heard it and vetoed it. Moving on to the next idea."

That was Madeleine's first indication that Garen's idea involved her participation. "Well, I haven't heard it yet."

"Let it go, dear," her husband growled.

"I haven't heard it, either," Agent Barella chimed in, earning a dark glare from Josh.

"Nor I," the others echoed.

Garen's smile was tight. "It would entail Antonio returning to the asylum to serve as bait. I'd send in Agent Michaelson to serve as a spiritual counselor to the patients and Mrs. Agent Michaelson to serve as the institution's newest laundress."

Lorelei's gasp echoed across the room. "You're sending her into the field already?"

"She's ready." Garen's expression was grim. "We all have our parts to play, and the Michaelsons' skill set is the most closely aligned with what we need on the inside."

"Good gracious," Jolene muttered. "This just got real."

Very real. Madeleine echoed her friend's sentiments inside her head. For the first time since she'd begun her training as an agent, she was thankful that Josh hadn't gone easy on her. It was the only reason she was ready for what came next.

Chapter 6: The Asylum

MADELEINE

QUESTIONS FLEW across the room so quickly for the next several minutes that it was all Josh and Garen could do to volley them.

The plan of action that emerged entailed staging what they would advertise as a major breakthrough in the cattle rustling case. It would be linked directly to Antonio's latest testimony. They'd spread the word that arrests were imminent and leak a short list of names that included several of Bando Brown's own associates. It would turn up the heat on him, so to speak, which would put Antonio back in Bando Brown's crosshairs.

The plan was dependent on Bando Brown subsequently taking action to silence the witness, this time for good. When he made his move, they would have a team in place to apprehend him.

"I'll do it." Antonio's easy capitulation more or less decided the matter.

"But it's so risky," Lorelai wailed. "Can't we find another way?"

"It's alright, lass," he soothed, glancing pointedly at her swollen belly. "I couldn't save my own daughter, but I can still save you and your babe. Brown has been targeting your ranch for months, and there are plenty more ranches on his hit list. He's not going to give up until he's either behind bars or in the ground."

"I'll do my part, as well." Madeleine felt like her less-than-glorious upbringing in the orphanage was finally going to pay off. A lifetime of hardship had made her tough enough to work at the asylum, not to mention her husband's recent and rigorous training.

"Madeleine!" her husband groaned.

"A promise is a promise," she reminded, catching and holding his gaze for an extended, emotion-charged moment. "I will always keep my promises, Josh. Every last one of them." She'd made some promises to him, as well, that she intended to keep — to have and to hold, to love and to cherish, 'til death.

THE NEXT SEVERAL days were a flurry of preparation as their team studied and trained for the next leg of their mission. Floor plans for the asylum were obtained and memorized.

When Garen was informed by the asylum that they'd recently hired two new laundresses already, he switched Madeleine's role to that of a nurse. She read a few medical textbooks and journals and practiced her fledgling skills on the other agents. He then hired a seamstress to commission a pastor's robe for Josh and a white nursing cap and cape for Madeleine. Lastly, Garen reached out to various legal contacts who arranged for a very public roundup of Antonio Dugal. He was subsequently returned to the asylum for confinement.

Lorelai wept openly as he was driven away in a cart with bars, truly concerned if she would ever see her most trusted ranch worker again. With her father, Clyde Woods, knocking on death's door due to a lung disease, Antonio had more or less stepped into a fatherly role in her life. Their relationship ran far deeper than that of an employer and employee.

"I'll bring him back to you," Madeleine promised later that evening. Lorelai and Jolene were helping her don her nursing uniform at the Broken Wheel Inn. With respect to Josh, who was watching the proceedings with a glower the entire time, they quickly said their goodbyes to give him as much time with his wife as possible before their departure.

He took much longer than she deemed necessary to adjust the collar of his robe in the mirror over the basin.

"One might claim that what you're doing is wife's job," she declared softly. As she watched him she smoothed the folds of her new and spotless white cloak.

He swung around to face her. "If I'd courted yo

the way you deserved in Missouri, would it have prevented us from reaching this crossroads?" There were shadows beneath his eyes and worry lines creasing the corners. He hadn't slept much since they'd begun their planning and preparation for their mission at the asylum.

"I've never lived by what-if's." Knowing he wouldn't find much comfort in her answer, Madeleine glided in his direction. Ignoring the uncertainties festering in the air, she slid her arms around his middle and rested her head against his shoulder. "I prefer to concern myself only with what is. This is what is. You and me. Us."

His arms came around her, and he pressed his cheek to the top of her head. "Along with the many risks associated with the upcoming mission."

"Risks that we'll be taking together," she reminded.

"I hope that's not supposed to make me feel better," he grumbled, "because it's not working."

She smiled against his shoulder. The fact that he was so disgruntled was all the more proof that he truly cared for her. "This probably won't make you feel any better, either, but I'm still going to say it. Given the choice, I would marry you and become a Pinkerton agent all over again. The life that we share is so much better than taking in washing and mending for a living."

"It's good to know you like me more than laundry," he responded dryly.

"I do," she assured, tipping her face up to his. "So much more."

His lips found hers. She melted into him, sliding her arms over his shoulders to wind them around his neck. Their mouths moved together, tenderly questing and sweetly cherishing.

"There's one last thing I'd like to get straight before we go." He lifted his head. "I want you to be mine, Madeleine Michaelson. Not just now, but also when the case is solved and beyond that." He anxiously searched her gaze as he awaited her response.

Her heart raced with joy at his words. "I am already yours, Josh. I swore my allegiance to the agency in Garen's office, but the vows I made to you are greater. Might I remind you that your ring is the one I'm wearing? Not the agency's."

Joy wafted across the hard angles and planes of his face. "You do not wish for an annulment, then?"

"I do not." It was an enormous relief to finally admit it. It was an even bigger relief to discover that he wanted to stay married, as well.

His arms tightened around her. "So, our union stands?"

"For as long as the Lord wills it."

"Thank you." Gazing deeply into her eyes, he slowly dipped his head closer to kiss her again.

She lingered in his embrace, reveling in the hope of a future together. There were still a thousand uncertainties ahead, but she was suddenly more confident about facing each and every one of them.

Josh reached between them to trace a finger down her cheek. "As a minister, I firmly believe that God's grace in our lives is sufficient, just like the Good Book says. But lately, I've wanted you by my side, as well. As my wife, partner, and best friend."

Every inch of her heart was drenched with adoration for him. *You are my biggest dream come true, Josh Michaelson!* "By your side is exactly where I want to be. Now and always."

"I am happy to hear it." He tipped his forehead against hers.

"Now let's go catch a criminal together," she urged.

"Right," he groaned and brushed his mouth against hers before letting her go.

FROM A DISTANCE, the trio of rectangular, gray stone buildings that comprised the Mercy's Road Asylum appeared to be perched on the rim of a canyon. As Madeleine's carriage drew closer, she could see they were actually set back a good hundred yards or more from the canyon's edge. A tall privacy fence enclosed the asylum grounds. Her driver brought the rig to a halt at the entrance gates, where a uniformed official greeted them and asked for their identification.

Madeleine handed a copy of her employment contract through the window. "I'm Nurse Caruthers," she informed the guard smoothly, hoping she sounded like a knowledgeable and confident medical professional. "Dr. Bloomingdale is expecting me." After much debate with her team mates, it had been decided she would revert to using her maiden name while working at the asylum.

He was the asylum's director. Garen Evans had managed to get a foot in the door at the asylum through a friend of a friend. It had resulted in both Madeleine and Josh being hired. The director wasn't aware of their true reason for coming to work at his facility, of course. As far as he knew, he'd simply gained two additional employees on short notice, for which he seemed grateful.

The asylum had been plagued with rapid turnover for the past couple of years. Though nobody seemed to be able to pinpoint the exact reason, employees rarely stayed for long. Most folks assumed it was due to the unsavoriness of working with some of the most damaged members of society. Madeleine suspected there was more to it, though, and she intended to get to the bottom of it soon.

She was posing as a nursing supervisor from an asylum in Missouri, a studious medical professional who'd purposely sought out the Mercy's Road Asylum in order to further her career. It was fortunate for the role she would be playing that their treatment program had recently been featured in two different medical journals.

The guard nodded at her papers and handed them back. "You'll find his office in the first building on the right, ma'am, first floor, second door to the left."

"Thank you, sir." Her driver dropped her off at the front entrance of the building, then helped her unload her travel bag and medical bag before driving off.

Tightly clasping the handles of both bags, she mounted the stone steps with apprehension swirling in her midsection. A high-pitched shout had her jogging to the far end of the veranda, where she could peer into the courtyard below. To her amazement, a dozen or so men and women roamed the park-like setting. They were dressed in solid white, like she was.

No, not exactly like me. They were patients. One was maneuvering himself around in a wheelchair. A few were strolling along a path paved with flat stones. Two women were reading side by side on a bench. A pair of men were hunched over a wine barrel table, playing a game.

"Welcome to the Mercy's Road Asylum." A quiet, cultured voice announced from behind her.

Madeleine spun around to face her first suspect on the case. She was under orders to consider all employees on site as suspects until she and Josh ruled them out.

The gentleman standing in front of her was a short, wraithlike creature. He was wearing a white lab coat over a pair of black trousers. Spectacles were perched on the end of his nose, through which he was studying her critically. "I am Dr. Bloomingdale. How may I help you, ma'am?"

The director himself. The very man I'm looking for. She could sense his irritation and impatience simmering just beneath the surface. Offering him her warmest smile, she announced brightly, "I am Nurse Caruthers. I am pleased to finally meet you in person, sir." She held out a hand.

He gave it the briefest of squeezes before dropping it. "The pleasure is all mine."

He was lying. Her gut told her that he took little pleasure in the encounter. Muffling a chuckle, she angled her head at the courtyard below. "What a beautiful, peaceful place this is!"

He gave her a curious, searching look. "That is the entire purpose of our existence. We provide moral, uplifting treatments to all our patients."

Unless her memory was at fault, he was quoting one of the journal articles word for word. *Nothing suspicious about that.* She nodded, still smiling.

"Not only do our patients find rest here, in a few rare cases, they've managed to achieve a full recovery."

Except for the occasional poor soul who's held here against their will at the wishes of a corrupt marshal. Madeleine struggled to maintain a neutral expression, wondering how in tarnation the man could be oblivious to such abuses happening right underneath his nose.

"I am honored to be joining such a reputable organization," she gushed. "I cannot wait to begin my duties, sir."

His answering smile was more of a grimace. "Your initial duties will be light, of course."

"But of course," she agreed smoothly. "I have much to learn. That is why I am here."

For a moment, suspicion clouded Dr. Bloomingdale's gaze. He quickly blinked it away. "I've never had the privilege of having my work observed before."

She nodded eagerly. "I am thrilled about the opportunity to learn from the best."

"Kind words, indeed." The doctor puffed out his chest a little. "Though you don't have the experience required to treat our most aggressive patients, the asylum is filled to capacity with milder cases. You'll not run out of patients to keep you busy while you strive to increase your skill level. That I can assure you." He beckoned her to follow him indoors. They walked together down a stark white hallway to his office.

She was struck at how bare the walls were, free of any paintings or other decorations.

Dr. Bloomingdale noted her puzzled look. "The sea of white has a calming effect on our patients," he explained. "Bright colors and designs would only make them anxious."

Madeleine nodded slowly, though she didn't entirely agree with his assessment. She could understand the use of calming colors and simplistic decor, but the complete absence of color didn't impress her as being all that therapeutic. It was so bland and boring that it gave her the fidgets. Then again, what did she know? She was neither a patient nor a real nurse.

Dr. Bloomingdale opened the door to his office, which turned out to be another set of plain white walls. The only adornments were a framed medical certificate behind his desk and a small green potted plant resting on the windowsill.

To her surprise, he did not offer her a seat. She set her bags on the floor and waited while he unlocked and opened his middle desk drawer.

Locked drawers, eh? Madeleine made a mental note of that interesting detail in the event it might prove useful to the case.

He produced a folder and handed it to her. "Included in this folder is a map of our facility."

"This is very helpful. Thank you," she murmured, opening the folder and scanning its contents.

"You're quite welcome, Nurse Caruthers. As you can see on the map, we have three patient wards, plus a dining area, gymnastics hall, library, music room, and chapel. The wings you'll have access to are unmarked. The ones marked out in red are off limits for safety reasons."

Her curiosity was piqued. "I very much appreciate your concern for my safety." She hoped to keep him talking.

"We are concerned for the safety of every employee, ma'am. The marked off areas are where our most severe cases are housed. Believe me, you would not wish to be caught wandering there alone."

"And where might my personal quarters be located?"

"On the third floor of the building we are currently standing in. The room number and key are taped to the inside flap of your folder."

"Wonderful! Thank you, sir." Though the third floor would offer her a modicum of privacy, it was a good distance away from the asylum's common areas. In a true emergency, she would have to rush down two flights of stairs to help out. That was assuming she'd even be able to hear any calls for assistance from that far away.

The director sighed and glanced at his watch. "Normally, I would spend more time with you on your first day. However, there's an urgent matter I must attend to right now. Perhaps we can continue your orientation over lunch?"

"Certainly, sir. I look forward to it."

"Excellent." He reached for another folder inside his desk, then relocked the drawer. "In the meantime, I ask that you quietly observe and do not interfere with the tasks of the other employees. Their work is difficult enough, as it is."

"I wouldn't dream of interfering." She was taken aback by his tone. "If I may ask, sir, what have you told them about me?"

"Very little." There was a sharp edge to his reply. "They're aware you're here to observe their work for a few weeks. That is all. We've had so many employees come and go lately. I did not wish to get their hopes up by promising them you'd stay. I'd rather wait and see how suited you are to the job."

A few weeks. It sounded like a warning to Madeleine — as if he wouldn't hesitate to terminate her employment if he deemed she was not suited to the job. Or, perhaps, if she dared call into question any of the shenanigans Antonio Dugal had reported about the place.

"What about the patients?" she inquired quietly. "May I interact with them while I observe them?" She'd been planning to converse with as many as possible in order to gather more information about the asylum.

"Certainly." Dr. Bloomingdale gave a careless wave. "Just don't upset them."

You, sirrah, could use a little work on your bedside manner. "I cannot wait to get started, sir."

"If you'll excuse me, Miss Caruthers." He brushed past her with his folder tucked beneath his arm. Something outside the window made him pause. "Ah. It appears our new chaplain has arrived. I shall quickly go introduce myself before heading to my meeting."

Her ears perked up at the announcement. It was comforting to know her husband was right on time. They'd purposely staggered their arrival times.

Surprised when Dr. Bloomingdale disappeared out the door, leaving her alone in his office, she quickly circled around his desk and attempted to search it. Every last drawer was locked. The only items displayed atop his desk were an ink well, pen, and a short stack of papers. The papers, as it turned out, contained a few invoices from local vendors — a baker, a cobbler, and an apothecary — as well as another map of the facility. She slipped the second map inside her folder, hoping he wouldn't miss it. She intended to compare it to the map he'd given her to ensure they were the same.

Then she gathered her bags and made her way back to the main hallway. As she searched for a stairwell leading upward, she passed more than a dozen plain white doors. Each one was punctuated by a small square window at eye level. A quick peek through a couple of them proved there were patients inside. They were mostly sleeping, but one was rocking aimlessly back and forth on his bed. Another was eating in solitude from a silver tray. It was a bit puzzling since Dr. Bloomingdale had mentioned there was a dining room on site.

All but one patient seemed oblivious to her presence. The man who was eating looked up and caught her eye. He immediately tossed his tray aside, spilling his peas and potatoes on the bed linens. Running to the door, he pounded it with his fists. "Let me out," he begged. "I did nothing wrong. I shouldn't be here. Please believe me, ma'am!"

She recoiled in horror. His words sounded so believable. His gaze appeared so lucid and clear.

"It never gets any easier, does it?" a sympathetic voice asked. "Beautiful creatures whose minds are wandering."

Madeleine turned to find a red-headed nurse about her age standing beside her. She'd not heard the woman approach. The sea of freckles on her pale fore-

111

head rippled across the wrinkles of concern there. "He's a few minutes overdue for his medications, I'm afraid. We had a nurse call out sick today, so we're running behind schedule. Not to worry, though. We'll have him calmed down in no time."

"I sure hope so!" Madeleine watched through the window as the nurse entered the patient's room and produced a syringe.

"No more shots, please!" The man tried to scoot away from her on his bed. "I shouldn't even be here. I'm but a simple farmer from Mercer. For pity's sake, I have a wife and children—" His shouts dissolved into a groan as he slumped back against his pillow. Eyes glazing with oblivion, he gazed up at the ceiling.

Madeleine's insides grew cold. According to Garen Evans, the little farming community of Mercer had been a hotbed of recent cattle rustling reports. The ranchers in that area were clamoring for a greater law enforcement presence to protect their livestock. So far, however, the sheriff of Mercer hadn't been able to deputize enough men to meet the need. Some of the ranchers had gone as far as to hire mercenaries to patrol the perimeter of the land. Ex-soldiers from both the United States and Mexico, if the rumors could be believed.

Madeleine pasted on what she hoped was an admiring smile as the nurse exited the patient's room. "I'm Nurse Caruthers, by the way. I'm new."

"I'm Nurse Weber." The woman's lips quirked in a welcoming smile.

AN AGENT FOR MADELEINE

"You did a marvelous job in there," Madeleine
prattled. "Is the patient new? He seemed particularly
anxious."

"Not at all." Nurse Weber looked amused by the
question. "Farmer Jim is a member of our century
club."

At Madeleine's puzzled expression, she explained.
"He's been at the asylum for more than a hundred
days. If he doesn't settle down soon, he'll be moved to
the D Ward for a few weeks of more specialized
treatments."

"Which are?" A sick feeling formed in the pit of
Madeleine's stomach as she recalled that Antonio had
been locked behind these same walls — not once, but
twice.

The nurse shrugged. "The usual stuff for more
severe patients. Shock treatments, restraints, increased
dosages of medications."

A thought struck Madeleine. "Why is it called the
D Ward? I thought Dr. Bloomingdale said there were
only three wards."

"That is correct." Nurse Weber made a comical
face. "It's nothing more than a jest, really. A Ward is for
the almost-normals. B is for the bedridden patients.
That's the ward we're in now. And D is for the worst
cases." She chuckled. "It used to be called the C Ward,
but one of the nurses renamed it D Ward, which she
claimed was short for Devil Ward. Anyhow, the name
stuck, and that's what everyone calls it now."

"This building is first in line," Madeleine mused,

making a mental note that Farmer Jim had been labeled as bedridden. "Why doesn't the A Ward come first?"

"Because every now and then, they rotate the patients. I'm not sure why. You'd have to ask the director."

"I will." She glanced at the woman's silver name tag and noted that it included the first initial of H.

"Please don't. I was merely jesting." Nurse Weber cast a worried look around them. "It's best not to ask too many questions around here, if you know what I mean."

No. Unfortunately, I don't. She nodded, pretending to understand. "Thank you for the advice."

"You're most welcome." The woman fluttered her fingers in farewell as she turned away. "I really hope you plan to stick around for a while, Nurse Caruthers."

"You may count on it," Madeleine called after her retreating figure. She continued on down the hall and finally located a stairwell at the far end. When she reached the third floor, she discovered several of the doors were missing their numbers. She had to silently count them in order to determine which one had been assigned to her. When she tried to enter it, her key stuck in the lock. She had to jiggle it for a while to open it.

Reaching the other side at long last, she dropped her bags inside the door and took a quick tour of their accommodations. It didn't take long, since the room wasn't much bigger than a broom closet. It contained a thin mattress on a simple wire frame, a washbasin in one corner, and two hooks on the wall for hanging garments. There was no tub or writing desk, no fireplace or other accoutrements. It brought to mind a jail cell. A single, narrow window overlooked the same courtyard she'd observed upon her arrival.

Swallowing her disappointment, Madeleine pulled out the folder Dr. Bloomingdale had given her and lounged against the windowsill with it. Inside, she found instructions about when and where she could dine and where she might bathe, if she so desired. *Of course, I desire to bathe, you old goat!*

She took the next few minutes to compare the marked up diagram of the asylum with the unmarked one she'd discovered on the director's desk. Her heartbeat quickened to note there was a C Ward, after all, though it was listed on the director's copy only — not the copy of the map she'd been given. *Interesting!* The C Ward was essentially the southern half of the D Ward. Meaning the B Ward came before the A Ward, and the C Ward came after D Ward.

What a peculiar numbering system! She could think of only one logical explanation for it. The asylum's layout was designed to hide certain patients.

A commotion outside her window had her whirling around to peer through the glass. In the courtyard below, a man was struggling to break free from two uniformed employees.

She unlatched her window and pushed it open so she could listen as well as watch.

"I'm not crazy, and you know it, you fools," the man bellowed. "I'm a farmer from Mercer, and when I get out of here..." His voice dwindled into silence as they dragged him indoors.

Madeleine's ears perked at the name of the man's hometown. It was the same as the one Farmer Jim was from. Her mind raced over everything she'd learned so far. Two men, both farmers from Mercer where there had recently been an uptick in cattle rustling activity, both claiming they weren't supposed to be at the facility. It didn't feel like a coincidence.

Moving across the room to her travel bag, she whipped out a sheet of stationery, along with her pen and inkwell, and jotted down what she'd discovered about Mercer. She was careful to record her notes, using the agency's pre-agreed-upon cypher. Now all she had to do was wander the halls until she had a "chance encounter" with the asylum's new chaplain. Then she'd slip the note to her husband, and he would ensure it was transported back to Garen Evans' office for further investigation by their team.

Chapter 7: Patient Witnesses

JOSH

JOSH WAS IMMEDIATELY STRUCK with how clean and peaceful the Mercy's Road Asylum appeared. One might've almost mistaken it for a quiet weekend retreat. His tour of the grounds was given by Dr. Bloomingdale, the asylum's director, a twitchy little man who kept checking his watch and mumbling about another important appointment on his calendar.

It sounded more like grumbling to Josh. *But what do I know?* It was way too soon to rule Dr. Bloomingdale in or out as a suspect.

There were breathtaking canyon views, courtyards, and gardens with meticulously maintained foliage. The place clearly employed a gardening staff.

"The outdoor space for patients here is truly remarkable." Josh nodded with approval. Compared to the more horrendous treatments of asylum patients in the past — heavy restraints and the like — he fully approved of a hospital where patients could enjoy a more humane existence. One designed to soothe and comfort instead of punish.

"Indeed, you'll find Mercy's Road Asylum superior to other facilities in nearly every way." Dr. Bloomingdale spoke with thinly veiled conceit, bordering on sarcasm. "We are much more forward-thinking. Our award-winning process for moral treatments is second to none."

It struck Josh as odd that the fellow didn't follow up his comments with any statistics concerning patient recovery rates. As a man of the cloth, Josh was far more concerned about the wellbeing of those confined to the facility than the number of awards resting inside some dusty display case.

They strolled together across a courtyard milling with patients. Their sloth-like movements and blank stares saddened Josh. What a desperate place for any person to be — a prisoner of one's own mind!

He wished he was at liberty to halt their tour of the asylum and pray for each and every one of them. However, he was on a case. It was best to finish interrogating the director first — discreetly, of course, so the director had no idea he was being questioned. There'd be plenty of time to encourage and counsel the patients later in the afternoon. Regardless of the criminal matters he was investigating, Josh planned to do exactly that.

"The patients appear drowsy." That was an understatement. To Josh, they appeared sedated to the point of being barely coherent. It was an alarming discovery for a place that advertised an environment that promoted rest and recovery. He hoped his comment would spark a conversation.

"Only because it's close to their nap time." The director's expression was taken aback. He clearly wasn't accustomed to criticism. "We follow a strict schedule, one that our patients find immense comfort in." His tone welcomed no further questions.

Nap time? For grown ups? Josh highly doubted the patients were lucid enough to have an opinion one way or the other about their routine. He decided to push the man's patience a little further, wanting to see what his reaction to the prospect of drawing some public attention on his hallowed institution would be.

"This is truly a lovely facility," he mused, scratching his chin as if lost in contemplation. "More like a resort than an asylum. It's no wonder you've been featured in so many magazines."

"Only two," Dr. Bloomingdale clarified tersely. "Both were medical journals. We don't make many headlines. In my experience, most folks would like to forget they live anywhere near an asylum."

Something a criminal could easily use to his or her advantage. "It's a shame." Josh nodded in sympathy. "You deserve more credit for the work you're doing here."

"We aren't looking for credit." Dr. Bloomingdale humbly inclined his head. "The comfort of our patients is all the thanks we need."

Though his words sounded kind on the surface, they certainly didn't explain how someone like Antonio Dugal had been confined as a patient against his will.

Josh held up a finger as if a thought had just occurred to him. "I might know a way to get more attention on the place. As it turns out, one of my friends is a journalist for the St. Louis Dispatch."

Dr. Bloomingdale made a scoffing sound. "If the locals couldn't care less about this place, why in the blazes would a bunch of out-of-towners?"

"I'm not finished." Josh grinned and closed in for his winning shot. "This friend happens to be the son of a prominent physician, one who happens to be writing a book on human diseases. What if I could convince him to add a chapter about your moral treatment program for mental illnesses? Naturally, he'd want to visit the place first and see the program for himself."

"I, er..." The director blinked and cleared his throat. "It's possible something could be arranged. However, he would need to come alone. We purposefully limit visitors to provide the least amount of disturbance to our patients and their treatments. I hold most of my interviews off site for this very reason."

All two of them, eh? "That's certainly understandable." It wasn't, of course. The fact that the man didn't welcome fellow clinicians to his facility was a warning flag to Josh. A true professional would have wanted to propagate his success in the hopes of his methods someday helping other patients at other facilities. Since that didn't seem to be on Dr. Bloomingdale's agenda, what *was* on his agenda?

When Josh fell silent, Dr. Bloomingdale's shoulders relaxed. "Whether or not I get to meet your friend, I very much appreciate your interest in spreading the word about the asylum. You've shown more interest in your first ten minutes here than most folks do in a lifetime."

"Your work speaks for itself, sir." Josh gazed around the courtyard with fawning admiration. "I could tell the moment I arrived, this campus was unique."

The director licked his lips and darted a sideways glance at Josh. "How so, reverend?"

Josh gave an affected laugh. "The shiny black Oldsmobile parked out front, for one thing. Climbing behind the wheel of a horseless carriage is high on my list of things to do before I die. Does it belong to you, doctor?" Josh was certain that the man's job as an asylum director didn't pay enough to afford such luxuries.

"I, ah...yes, it belongs to me." Dr. Bloomingdale bobbed his head, looking singularly uncomfortable. "Always dreamed of owning one." He stuck a finger in the front of his collar and tugged it away from his throat. "If it weren't for an inheritance from a great-uncle, I never could've afforded it."

Josh tucked away that bit of information to pass on to Garen. It would be interesting to see if Dr.

Bloomingdale's story about a deceased relative checked out, or if his inflow of funds was coming from a different source. There was no missing the ruby signet ring on the director's pinky finger or the diamonds winking from his cuff links.

"Well, hello, Dr. Bloomingdale!" The sound of his wife's cheery voice had Josh's insides tensing with both joy and concern on her behalf. This was her first assignment as an agent. He would've preferred it to be anywhere but inside an insane asylum.

"Hello, ma'am." The director's voice was brittle. "I trust you're getting settled in?"

"I'm trying to, sir. I met Nurse Weber and observed her administer medicine to a patient. However, it's such a beautiful day that I couldn't resist taking a turn around the courtyard."

Dr. Bloomingdale's lips flatlined. "Nurse Caruthers is a nursing supervisor from another facility, who's come to observe my work," he explained in a tight voice. He gave a rigid nod in Josh's direction for Madeleine's benefit. "Pastor Josh Michaelson is our new pastoral counselor, ma'am."

"A pleasure to meet you, ma'am." Josh held out his hand to her and was startled to feel a slip of paper pressed against his palm. His wife had only arrived an hour or so ahead of him. He'd not expected her to write up her first report so quickly.

"It's very nice to meet you, as well, Pastor Michaelson. It's my first day here," she babbled on, "but I plan to make it by the chapel soon."

"Come by any time, ma'am." He inclined his head at her and covertly watched the sway of her slender figure as she walked away.

With her white-blonde hair and luminous blue eyes, his wife was the most beautiful woman he'd ever met. The very sight of her never failed to make his heart pound. He stuck the note she'd delivered in the pocket of his robe and allowed the director to bring their tour to a swift conclusion.

Only after he was locked inside his new office at the chapel did he unfold the note and decipher it. What he read made his blood chill. Apparently, Bando Brown was using the Mercy's Road Asylum to sideline anyone who got in the way of his criminal operations. More than likely he was paying Dr. Bloomingdale hush money to buy his cooperation.

Anxious to get this new information to Garen, he headed to the dining hall early for supper. Agent Edgar Barella had managed to secure a position as a delivery driver for a grocer.

The dining hall was as large as a church sanctuary and crammed with round tables. Four to five chairs circled each one. By Josh's estimate, the room could easily seat fifty or more patients. However, less than two dozen were present. Several weren't bothering to eat. They were simply picking at their food or staring into space. One scrawny fellow was tearing off small bits from his toast and tossing them to the floor as if he was feeding an imaginary flock of birds.

A pair of nurses wove their way around the tables,

stopping now and then to tend to a patient. Three other nurses were seated, feeding patients who required assistance.

Josh nodded at a nurse standing a few feet away, a grandmotherly woman with her hair twisted back in a tidy bun, as he lifted a tray from the stack at the beginning of the food line. There was only one patient in front of him, a man moving very slowly because he kept stopping to rearrange the silverware on his tray. Josh watched in fascination as the fellow meticulously lined up his fork to the right of his spoon. As soon as he was finished lining them up, he swapped their order and proceeded to realign his fork to the left of his spoon.

As Josh stepped closer, he could hear the man muttering, "Shouldn't even be here. As the Lord is my witness..."

"Come along, Flynn. There are others in line, hon." The gray-haired nurse swooped in and gently guided him toward a nearby table. With her hands on his shoulders, she nudged him into his chair.

"That's Farmer Flynn to you, young-un," he grumbled, but he obligingly lifted his fork and started eating.

Another farmer, eh? Naturally, Josh wondered if he happened to be from Mercer like the others his wife had mentioned in her note. Noting the extra seats at the fellow's table, he decided to join him and find out.

As he made his way through the rest of the food line, he kept an eye out for Edgar Barella. The agent was supposed to make his first appearance this evening during a food delivery.

While he scanned the room, he greeted and made small talk with the two ladies in aprons serving food. Both stirred and ladled food with quick, efficient movements. Today's main entrée was chicken and dumplings.

"You must be the new chaplain," the first one greeted him with a curious glance at his robe.

"Guilty as charged." He inclined his head respectfully, making her chuckle. "Pastor Josh Michaelson, at your service." He swiped an apple and a banana from the fruit bowl to his left.

"Well, I'm Maude. Just Maude." She ladled a generous serving of dumplings into a bowl for him and handed it across the counter.

Josh's stomach growled as he set it on his tray. Out of the corner of his eye, he finally spied Agent Barella peeking his head around the corner from the back storage room.

There you are, you scoundrel! "Blast it all," Josh muttered as he deliberately dropped his apple and sent it rolling down the serving food line in Edgar's direction.

"Some days I have ten thumbs," he grumbled. With a wry smile at Maude, he left his food tray on the counter and jogged after the stray apple. Pretending not to see him, Edgar dove for it, as well. Their hands closed over the apple at the same time, Madeleine's note exchanged hands, and the two men came up

laughing ruefully and rubbing their heads as if they'
bumped into each other while they were down there.

THE TEAM of Pinkerton agents worked in tander
for the next several days — identifying and cataloguin
patients, exploring the facility, and gathering evidenc
that would hopefully lead to a search warrant of th
compound.

Madeleine was able to visit the chapel three tim
during her first week there. During each visit, sh
headed down to the altar to pray. Under the guise c
blessing and anointing her, Josh stole a few hast
conferences with her. On Friday, her report was trul
alarming.

"Nurse Weber allowed me to give Farmer Jim h
medication. He never cooperates for his treatment
and today was no exception. He was lucid when w
spoke. And did he ever have a story to tell!" She drew
shaky breath. "We were right, Josh. About everything.

His hand froze while tracing the sign of the cro
on her forehead. "Oh?"

"He's willing to serve as a witness in court. C
whatever else it takes to restore him to his family."

Josh's hand started moving again. He mechanical
finished tracing the cross on his wife's forehead. Wh
he really wanted to do was take her some place sa
until the danger was past. However, she'd served a vit
role in cracking the case. Her detective skills we

impeccable. Because of her, a decent number of farmers and ranchers were finally going to get the justice they deserved. Husbands would be restored to their wives, cattle would be returned to their rightful owners, and outlaws would be placed behind bars where they belonged.

Instead of snatching up his wife and running, Josh closed his eyes and quietly entreated the Lord for protection over her and the rest of their fellow agents.

Her head remained bowed so long after his prayer ended that he bent his head over hers again. "Are you alright, sweetheart?"

"Yes," she whispered.

"It's time," he rasped. Time for her to go keep an eye on their witnesses while the rest of their team prepared for the coming raid.

She still didn't raise her head. "I love you, Josh," she whispered. "I love you so much that it scares me."

Her confession rendered him speechless. Yes, he'd longed to hear words of love from her someday, but why now? Was it because she was afraid she might not get another chance to tell him?

When she raised her head, however, there was no fear radiating from her striking blue gaze. She drenched him with a smile that went straight to his heart.

The wind left his chest. *My precious wife!* He hoped she could read the blind adoration in his gaze, because he couldn't figure out what had happened to his voice.

All he could do was watch her with helpless longing as she stood and swept past him up the aisle.

AS SOON AS Garen Evans received word of Farmer Jim's willingness to witness against his captors, he leaked the story he and his team had previously concocted about a breakthrough in the case. It went to every newspaper in a hundred-mile radius. He expected most of them would print it the next morning. Then he worked with local law enforcement to secure a search warrant for the asylum. The Pinkertons would join forces with them to surround the facility at first light, waiting for Bando Brown to make his move to silence the witnesses once and for all.

The prayers Josh uttered next were the most heartfelt of his career. "Be with us, Lord God. Give us wisdom, strength, and protection during the coming raid. Guide our rescue efforts, and help us deliver justice to those who deserve it. Amen."

He couldn't wait until the case was closed. He wanted nothing more than to have his wife back in the shelter of his arms. And when that moment came, he was finally going to tell her everything that was on his heart.

No more holding back.

Chapter 8: Justice All Around

MADELEINE

MORNING BROKE with a blast of hot, dry wind. Over the distant mountain peaks, a sand storm raged, dark and ugly, though it didn't show any indication of heading their way.

Yet.

According to the locals, the weather was peculiar in this area. It could change in a heartbeat.

The morning sun bathed the three long buildings of the Mercy's Road Asylum with a rosy red glow, turning the uniforms of the patients in the courtyard from white to pink.

Madeleine stepped away from the window overlooking the asylum grounds with a shudder of discomfort. She couldn't wait to leave the lumpy mattress in her room behind and return to her much bigger and nicer bed at the boarding house.

Most of all, she couldn't wait to be reunited with her husband. Her face heated at the thought.

Ever since her passionate confession of love to him yesterday, she'd been consumed with regret. What had she been thinking, blurting out her feelings like that to him? To her intense mortification, he hadn't said a word in return. He'd only stared at her with a stunned expression in his gorgeous, coffee-colored eyes. She'd not been able to escape the chapel fast enough afterward.

They'd only been married a few weeks. She should have waited to tell him how much she loved him. It was too soon. Their relationship needed more time to develop and grow first.

Not only was she madly in love with the man, she was consumed with fear for his safety today. Yes, he was armed and experienced. Gracious, but she had proof of that firsthand! He'd been merciless in his training with her in recent days. He could run, shoot, and dodge bullets all at the same time. He was also a master negotiator, assuring her it was possible to talk one's way out of a dangerous situation without firing a single bullet.

Wouldn't it be amazing if Bando Brown could be collared without any bloodshed? She wasn't holding her breath, though. He and his band of outlaws were the most dangerous men she'd ever encountered.

Madeleine dressed with haste, buttoning her cloak with trembling fingers. Her bags were packed, as well. Today was her last day on the job, regardless of the outcome of the raid. She'd already turned in her notice to Dr. Bloomingdale. Before leaving the room, she stood in front of the basin mirror, trying to regulate her breathing.

I can do all things through Christ who strengthens me. She repeated the age-old scripture inside her head until the shaking in her knees subsided. She would be of no use to her team if she walked down the stairs in an emotional tizzy. As one of only three detectives on the premises, she had a crucial role to play.

I will not let them down!

Antonio and the other patients, who were confined against their will, were very much depending on her protection. She was armed; they were not. If Bando Brown believed the breaking news story about a major breakthrough in the case, it was very likely he would pay a visit to the asylum soon. There were too many men here who could serve as witnesses against him. Madeleine was honestly surprised he'd kept them alive this long.

Shoving her packed bags beneath her bed, she let herself out the door and made her way to the stairwell. Dr. Bloomingdale met her in the hallway as she descended the final stretch of stairs.

"Nurse Caruthers!" He glanced in agitation around them. "I, er, thought you'd left already."

Her eyebrows flew upward. "I reckon I'll be on my way after lunch, sir. Today is my last day."

"I thought yesterday was supposed to be your last day." He grabbed her elbow and tugged her roughly down the hallway. To her dismay, they were heading in the opposite direction of Antonio Dugal's room, where she was supposed to be stationed.

"Dr. Bloomingdale," she gasped, wrenching her arm from his. "I am able to walk on my own."

"I beg your pardon, ma'am." He glanced nervously over his shoulder.

She did the same and caught sight of a masked man backing out of sight. Either that, or her imagination was playing tricks on her. "What is going on, sir?" Since he showed no signs of letting her return to her duties, she figured she might as well get him to talk.

He turned to study her for a moment. Without warning, he reached for her left hand and lifted it to examine her wedding ring. "Take it off," he snarled.

"Dr. Bloomingdale!" Though her heart raced with apprehension, she pretended indignation, staring at him as if he'd lost his mind.

His voice gentled a few degrees. "I need to see what's engraved inside the setting."

"It's the most ridiculous thing anyone has ever asked of me, but if you insist..." Still scowling at him, she gave a grunt of exertion, feigning difficulty in wrenching the ring from her finger. She slapped it into his palm with a huff of anger.

She inwardly rejoiced at the fact that Josh had insisted on replacing her agency ring with a family heirloom. There was nothing tying her beautiful emerald to the Pinkerton agency.

Dr. Bloomingdale held it up to the light and squinted at the setting. "Harrumph! I was so sure you were one of them." He handed it back to her with a snort of derision.

"One of whom, sir?" Her voice was crisp as she slid the ring back on her finger.

"Never mind that, Nurse Caruthers. All you need to know is that we have a dangerous situation on our hands. For your own safety, I need you to depart the campus." He gave her a hard look. "Immediately."

What a pack of lies! Madeleine was more certain than ever that the director was up to his eyeballs in Bando Brown's criminal activities. She could tell by his pallor that he was scared, though. Maybe he wasn't as cooperative as she'd originally believed him to be.

"What is it, Dr. Bloomingdale?" She adopted a quiet voice that invited his confidence. "I know I'm not trained to deal with the toughest patients, but I'm a very capable nurse. Just tell me how I can help."

A shot sounded in the distance, making them both spin back in the direction of Antonio Dugal's room.

Without waiting for the director's permission, Madeleine sprinted down the hall toward the sound.

"Stop, Miss Caruthers! You cannot go down there!"

She could hear his pounding footfalls behind her.

She arrived at the door of Antonio's room and managed to hunker behind the arched inset of the door frame just as the second shot sounded. Dr. Bloomingdale flew her way, nearly crashing into her. His expression livid, he grasped her shoulders while a trio of masked men converged on them.

"I tried to warn you," he growled.

Armed deputies and Pinkerton agents crept up behind the three masked men, tackling them to the floor. Madeline watched as Josh, Edgar, and John helped subdue the prisoners and drag them out of sight. All of this happened in seconds with no weapons fired, leaving Madeleine alone with Dr. Bloomingdale once again.

"You *are* one of those blasted agents, aren't you?" he accused.

"I have no idea what you're talking about," she gasped, adopting an indignant expression once again.

"Oh, but you do, Miss Caruthers. I can see it in your eyes," he sighed as he removed a silver pistol from his pocket.

She nervously eyed his movements. "You don't have to do this, Dr. Bloomingdale."

"Clearly, you have no idea what sort of men we're up against."

What sort of men we're up against. She repeated his words inside her head. *He said we.* "Oh, but I do, sir, and you're not one of them."

He'd not started out that way, at any rate. She'd done her homework. By now, she knew just about everything there was to know about the crotchety old director. Drawing a deep breath, she continued, "I know you have a lovely wife and two beautiful daughters. I know you worked hard to build this cutting-edge facility and that you really do believe those who are ill in their minds can be made well again through proper treatment." She kept her voice carefully modulated, infusing it with both admiration and concern. "That's what you used to believe, at any rate. When did that change, sir?"

His expression twisted with despair. "It didn't change, Miss Caruthers, but my circumstances did. Someone found out how ill my wife was and how far behind I was on the payments for her medical treatments."

"Who found out, Dr. Bloomingdale?"

At his stony silence, she pressed, "Was Bando Brown the one who paid you to confine patients against their will?"

He stared at her in horror. "How did you—?"

"Say no more, director. You can step aside now. I'll handle this one."

Madeleine's heart lurched with dread at the coldness in the voice of the man approaching them. She knew without asking that she was in the presence of the dirty U.S. Marshal.

She watched Dr. Bloomingdale give a fearful nod and dash off like a scared puppy with his tail between his legs. He didn't stand a chance at making it off the grounds as a free man. Garen Evans had already traced the hush money to a series of bank accounts in his name. He was going to jail for his part in the criminal operation.

Which didn't make Madeleine's current situation any less precarious. She'd never before heard the raspy male voice resounding off the walls of the otherwise empty corridor. However, it contained the slight lisp Antonio Dugal had described.

The corrupt marshal looked nothing like the man she'd pictured. He was shorter, for one thing, and far more innocent looking. His plain features and mousey hair were unremarkable. His expression, however, was devoid of all human emotion.

"It's over, Mr. Brown," she informed in a voice that was much calmer than she felt. "There are more witnesses to your cattle rustling scheme than you can shake a stick at. You might as well lay down your weapon. No one else needs to get hurt, including you."

He chuckled mirthlessly and continued to advance on her.

A tiny clicking sound to her right was her only indication that Antonio had broken free of his cell.

"What are you doing?" she hissed without moving her lips. It was another trick her husband had taught her.

"Saving you," he whispered.

Since Bando Brown's expression didn't change, she could only surmise he hadn't yet caught sight of Antonio. From the corner of her eye, she saw the glint of a gun in his hands. Who in heaven's name had supplied a patient with a weapon?

"I don't need saving," she hissed. "Just let me do my job."

"This is my fight, ma'am. Not yours." His voice was flat with determination. He'd waited a long time for this day to come.

"No," she pleaded, trying one last time to reason with him as the dirty marshal's boots stomped closer.

Without another word, Antonio leaped in front of her and opened fire.

Seconds later, two figures lay motionless on the floor. Then the building erupted into pandemonium.

BOTH MEN WERE CARTED off for medical treatment. From what Madeleine understood, both were in critical condition. It was unclear if they would pull through.

She mightily hoped they did, even ex-Marshal Brown — *especially* ex-Marshal Brown. He deserved to face a judge and jury for the many crimes he'd committed and all the families he'd wronged in the process. He deserved to face the punishment he had coming.

She and her team of fellow agents worked the next several hours alongside the sheriff of Midland Hills and his deputies to process all the victims and record all the witness statements. In the end, it was determined that a grand total of eleven patients were being held against their will at the Mercy's Road Asylum. Interestingly enough, they were from six different towns.

Apparently, Bando Brown had been using the asylum for quite some time as a means to blackmail, extort money, and otherwise punish the farmers and ranchers who dared to oppose his cattle rustling activities.

The witness statements would be highly instrumental in the coming weeks to make more arrests. Bando Brown's network of criminals was extensive. It wouldn't be entirely disbanded in a day, but it *would* come toppling down, thanks to the hard work of the Pinkerton agents in both the Bull County and Midland Hills offices.

It was with immense exhaustion and exhilaration that Madeleine returned with her husband to the Broken Wheel Inn at the end of the day. She removed her nurse's cap at long last and tossed it on the bed. Then she unbuttoned her cape.

"I could sleep for a year," she declared, folding her cape and setting it atop her travel bag. She'd kept up a steady stream of chatter during the entire buggy ride back to the inn, anything to fill the awkward silence between the two of them. He'd watched her with an inscrutable expression and hadn't added more than a handful of words to the conversation.

It was probably too much to hope that he'd forgotten her ill-timed declaration of love. It didn't mean she couldn't work to restore a light and casual air between them, though.

He removed his chaplain robe and hung it on one of the hooks against the wall. Beneath it, he was wearing denim trousers, boots, and a white shirt with the sleeves rolled up.

Madeleine observed him from beneath her lashes,

thinking he looked a million shades of wonderful. He was strong, capable, and breathtakingly gorgeous. She had no doubt whatsoever that all the wisdom and training he'd poured into her had kept her alive back at the asylum.

When he finally turned to face her, concern was stamped across his handsome features. "May we please skip the rest of the small talk, Mrs. Michaelson?"

Her eyelashes fluttered against her cheeks as he strode in her direction. "I, ah, certainly. Would you rather discuss the case? It was quite an ordeal, wasn't it?"

"No." He reached for her, sliding his arms around her to pull her close. "I'd rather discuss you." He bent his head to look her straight in the eye. "Our marriage, to be more specific."

She flushed, wanting to dissolve straight through the floor. "If this is about what I so foolishly blurted out yesterday, I—"

"I love you, too, Madeleine."

Her eyes widened in shock. "Josh!" She couldn't bear the thought of him making a false claim in order to spare her feelings. She was well aware that she cared more for him than he cared for her, and she could live with that. At the moment, she was just grateful they'd both survived the dangers of the raid on the asylum. "You don't have to say anything you don't really feel. I—"

"I love you, Madeleine," he repeated firmly, "and

I'm going to keep telling you that until you believe me."

Her eyes misted at the fervor in his voice. Oh, how she wanted to believe such a miracle was possible, but it was a little hard to swallow, everything considered.

However, he wasn't near finished, it seemed. "I love you so much that I had trouble breathing all morning, just thinking about all the risks you were taking to fulfill your role in the case."

"I was worried about you, too," she confessed softly.

"But," he reached between them to lightly tap the tip of her nose, "I never doubted you were going to do your job and do it well."

Her insides melted. "Thank you, Josh." A compliment from him was worth more than a fortune in gold.

He shuddered and cuddled her closer. "That said, I had to lean on my faith in ways I've never had to before, when the bullets started flying."

Confusion flooded her at the fierce look in his eyes and the tenderness of his touch. "If you truly love me, then why didn't you say so back in the chapel?"

He shook his head helplessly at her. "Because you stole the breath right out of my chest. If you'd stuck around even a minute longer, I would've said the words back. We might've never finished solving the case, though, because I would have been too busy doing this."

He bent closer to seam his mouth to hers.

The rest of Madeleine's uncertainties dissolved

beneath the sweet ambush of his kisses. With a soft sigh of wonder, she wound her arms around his neck and kissed him back.

When he raised his head, the light in the room was fading, and the first stars were studding the sky on the other side of the window.

"My dearest Madeleine," Josh said huskily. "I can't promise you a future without more danger — not in our line of business. I've long since given up that castle in the clouds. What I can promise is that I'll gladly spend the rest of my life at your side, saving souls and fighting crime together, if you're willing."

"I'm willing," she assured breathlessly. She cupped his face in her hands and sealed the promise with another heart-shaking kiss.

Saving souls and solving crimes with a man who loved her to distraction was more than she'd ever dreamed of. *Good gracious!* It was a thousand times better than spending the rest of her days as a laundress. She seriously couldn't wait to see what the mighty Pinkertons had in store for them next!

---

*I hope you enjoyed **An Agent for Madeleine**!*

WESTERN BRIDES UNDERCOVER
Read them all!
An Agent for Bernadette
An Agent for Lorelai

An Agent for Jolene
An Agent for Madeleine

Then keep turning the page for a sneak peek at
Mail Order Brides of Cowboy Creek #1
Cowboy for Annabelle.

Much love,
Jovie

Sneak Preview: Cowboy for Annabelle

MAIL ORDER BRIDES ON THE RUN

TO PROTECT *her from a ruthless set of debt collectors, an impoverished southern belle agrees to become the mail-order bride of a rugged cowboy.*

After refusing to marry the cruel new owner of her childhood home, Annabelle Lane finds herself on the run from the scoundrels he hires to change her mind. In desperation, she signs a mail-order bride contract and hops on the next train, praying the groom she is matched with is a man worth running toward.

The most sought-after range rider in the west, Ethan Vasquez is highly skilled at protecting livestock from bears, wolves, and rustlers. But it's a job that leaves no time for courting, no matter how determined he is to have a family of his own someday. When a dare from friends has him scrambling to send off for a mail-order bride, he never imagines how quickly she will arrive or how much trouble will follow. It's a good thing he knows a thing or two about handling predators. He can only hope she finds his heavily scarred hands worth joining with hers in holy matrimony after the first wave of danger is past.

Grab your copy in eBook, paperback, or Kindle Unlimited on Amazon!
Cowboy for Annabelle

MAIL ORDER BRIDES ON THE RUN
Read them all!
Cowboy for Annabelle
Cowboy for Penelope
Cowboy for Eliza Jane

Much love,
Jovie

Free Book!

Don't forget to join my mailing list to be the first to know about new releases, free books, special discount prices, Bonus Content, and giveaways.

https://BookHip.com/GNVABPD

Note From Jovie

Guess what? I have some Bonus Content for you. Read a little more about the swoony cowboy heroes in my books by signing up for my mailing list.

There will be a special Bonus Content chapter for each new book I write, just for my subscribers. Plus, you get a FREE book just for signing up!

Thank you for reading and loving my books.

Joyce

Join Cuppa Jo Readers!

If you're on Facebook, you're invited to join my group, Cuppa Jo Readers. Saddle up for some fun reader games and giveaways + book chats about my sweet and swoony cowboy book heroes!

https://www.facebook.com/groups/CuppaJoReaders

Sneak Preview: Grace

MAIL ORDER BRIDES OF COWBOY CREEK

A long-lost soldier, a sister of the woman he was once engaged to, and the merry mischief of a Christmas matchmaker...

GRACE BYRD HAS BEEN in love with Lieutenant Charley Arrington for as long as she can remember, but he barely notices her existence when her oldest sister, Elizabeth, is around. Grace's heart is shattered when he goes missing in action and is presumed dead. She silently vows to live out her days as a spinster, because she cannot imagine ever giving her heart to another man.

Now he's back in their lives — returned from a southern hospital where he suffered from amnesia for months. Ready to claim her oldest sister's hand in marriage at long last, he quickly learns Elizabeth has become a mail-order bride in his absence, to help out with her family's failing finances. What's more, she's fallen in love with her new husband.

Is this Grace's second chance to win the heart of the man she loves? Can Charley move beyond his old dreams and replace them with new ones? One-click this sweet, small town romance to find out...and be whisked away by the hope and healing of the holidays!

Grab your copy in eBook, paperback, or Kindle Unlimited on Amazon!
Grace

MAIL ORDER BRIDES OF COWBOY CREEK
Complete trilogy — read them all!
Elizabeth
Grace
Lilly

Much love,
Jovie

Preview: Hot-Tempered Hannah

BOOK #1 IN THE MAIL ORDER BRIDES
RESCUE SERIES

UNLIKE HIS NAME SUGGESTED, there
was nothing angelic about Gabriel Donovan. Quite
the contrary. While most men were settled down with
a wife and family by his ripe old age of twenty-six, he
preferred the life of a bounty hunter, tracking and
rounding up men who carried a price on their heads.
He extracted money and information and taught an
occasional lesson to particularly deserving scoundrels
when circumstances warranted it.

Most people kept their distance from him, and he
was okay with that. More than okay. Making friends
wasn't part of the job, and he sincerely hoped he didn't
run into anyone he knew at the Pink Swan tonight.
Unlike the other patrons, he wasn't looking for enter-
tainment to brighten the endless drag of mining activities in windy Headstone, Arizona. If any of the show
girls from the makeshift stage at the front of the room
bothered to approach him, they'd be wasting their

time. He'd purposefully chosen the dim corner table for its solitude. All he wanted was a hot meal and his own thoughts for company.

"Why, if it isn't Gunslinger Gabe," a female voice cooed, sweet as honey and smoother than a calf's hide. She plopped a mug of watered down ale on the table, scraping the metal cup in his direction. "I's beginning to worry you wasn't gonna show up for your Friday night supper."

"Evening, Layla." He hated her use of his nickname. Hated how the printed gazettes popping up across the west ensured he would never outride the cheeky title. It followed him from town to town like an infection. He hated it for one reason: None of his eight notorious years of quick draws and crack shots had been enough to save his partner during that fated summer night's raid.

It was a regret that weighed down his chest every second of every day like a ton of coal. It was a regret he would carry to his grave.

He nodded at the waitress who leaned one hand on the small round table with chipped black paint.

"Well, what's it going to be this time, cowboy?" Her dark eyes snapped with a mixture of interest and impatience. "Bean stew? Mutton pie? As purty as your eyes are, I got other tables to wait on, you know."

The compliment never failed to disgust him. Along with his angelic name, he'd been told more times than he cared to count that he'd been gifted with innocent features. If he heard another word about his clear, lake-blue eyes that inspired trust, he would surely vomit.

"Surprise me." He hoped to change the subject. Both entrees sounded equally good to him. He was hungry enough to eat the pewter serving ware, if she didn't hurry up with his order.

Layla's movements were slow as sap rolling down the bark of a maple tree. "If it's a surprise you're looking for...." She swayed a step closer.

"Bring me both," he said quickly. "The stew and the pie. I haven't eaten since this morning."

"Fine." The single word was infused with a world of derisive disappointment. A few steps into her stormy retreat, she spun around. Anger rippled in waves across her heart-shaped face. "I know what you really want."

"You do?" The question grated out past his lips before he could recall the words. Sarcastic and challenging. It had been a rough day. The last thing he needed was a saloon wench to whip out her crystal ball and presume to know anything about his life. Or his longings. No one this side of the grave could fill the void in his heart.

"I sure do, cowboy." She was back in front of him before he could blink, her scarlet dress shimmering with her movements. "An' I can show you a real special time. Something you ain't never gonna find on no supper menu."

He didn't figure any good would come of trying to explain that his heart belonged to a ghost. Wracking his brain for a sensible way to end their conversation without offending her further, he stared drearily at his mug. There was no quickening of his breathing around any women these days. No increased thump of his heartbeat. Not like there had been with Hannah. His dead partner. Or Hot-Tempered Hannah, as she'd been known throughout the west.

Then again, maybe he wasn't completely dead yet on the inside. He felt a stirring in the sooty, blackened, charred recesses of his brain as his memories of her sprang back to life. Memories that refused to die.

His mind swiftly conjured up all five feet three inches of her boyishly slender frame stuffed in men's breeches along with the tumultuous swing of red hair she'd refused to pin up like a proper lady. Nor could he forget the taunting tilt of her head and the voice that turned from sweet to sassy in a heartbeat, a voice that had been silenced forever due to his failure to reach their rendezvous in time.

So help him, he was finally feeling something alright — a sharp gushing hole of pain straight through the chest. He mechanically reached for his glass and downed the rest of his ale in one harsh gulp.

"Well, I'll be!" The waitress peered closer at him, at first with amazement then with growing irritation. "I've been around long enough to know when a body's pining for someone else."

What? Am I that transparent? His brows shot up and he stared back, thoroughly annoyed at her intrusive badgering.

Layla was the first to lower her eyes. "Guess I'll get back to work, since you're of no mind to chat." Her frustration raised her voice to a higher pitch. "I was jes' trying to be friendly, you unsociable cad. I'll try not to burn your pie or spill your soup, since that's all you be wanting." Her voice scorched his ears as she pivoted in a full circle and stormed in the direction of the kitchen.

He stared after her, wishing he could call her back but knowing his apology wouldn't make her feel any better. A woman scorned was a deadly thing indeed. He could only hope she didn't poison his supper.

He hunched his shoulders over his corner table and went back to reminiscing about his dead partner. Known as Hot-Tempered Hannah throughout Arizona, she'd stolen his heart with a single kiss then threatened to shoot him if he ever tried to steal another.

He had yet to get over her. Hadn't looked at another woman since. She was three months in the grave, and he was nowhere near moving on with his life.

Layla stomped back in his direction twice. Once to refill his mug and several minutes later to dump his tray on the table with such a clatter that a few droplets of stew spilled over the edge of the bowl.

"A man at one of the faro tables paid me to deliver you a message," she snapped. "He wants you to stick around 'til he's finished dealing. Says he needs to speak with you 'bout somethin' important."

The drowsy contentedness settling in Gabe's bones from the hot meal sharpened back to full awareness. He paused in the act of lifting a spoonful of stew to his mouth. "Which man?"

She pointed to the nearest gaming table. "Over there. The one dealing."

Technically, the man was shuffling, but he pushed back his Stetson an inch and deliberately nodded a greeting in response to their curious stares. Gabe didn't recognize him. They were dressed much the same, albeit Gabe hadn't bothered to remove his trench coat like the other man had.

His keen bounty hunter eyes zeroed in on the ridge of concealed weapons beneath the man's vest. Most people wouldn't have noticed, but Gabe wasn't most people. He was well paid to notice everything around him. The things people wanted him to notice and the things they preferred he didn't.

Those same sensory nodes told him Layla was still present, though she was standing behind him not making a peep. His gaze remained fixed on his summoner. "Does this faro dealer have a name?"

She sniffed. "He didn't say, and I ain't takin' extra to find out. He's working a little too hard for my tastes to fit in, if you know what I mean."

Gabe knew exactly what she meant and was surprised enough at her perception to spare her a glance. He reached in his pocket, and she tensed. He slid an extra bill in her direction across the scratched up tabletop. Something told him she could use the money. "Thanks for passing on the gentleman's message."

The frown on her lacquered lips eased. "Maybe some time you and I can visit a little longer, gunslinger?" She batted her lashes at him.

He highly doubted it — ever. "Dinner tastes wonderful. I thank you for that as well." He returned his hand to his soup spoon and his attention to the faro dealer. Something told him he was about to receive a new bounty assignment.

Layla lingered a few moments longer but finally left him on a drawn-out sigh of resignation.

He ate quickly while observing the card game. In seconds, he determined the game was rigged. Unlike most tables where the odds generally leaned in the banker's favor, this table broke even every few rounds. The intervals were entirely too regular to be coincidental. If Gabe's suspicions were correct, the faro dealer wasn't making a penny. *Very odd.*

Grab your copy in eBook, paperback, or Kindle Unlimited on Amazon!
Hot-Tempered Hannah

Complete series — read them all!
Hot-Tempered Hannah
Cold-Feet Callie
Fiery Felicity

Misunderstood Meg
Dare-Devil Daisy
Outrageous Olivia
Jinglebell Jane
Absentminded Amelia
Bookish Belinda
Tenacious Trudy
Meddlesome Madge
Mismatched MaryAnne
MOB Rescue Series Box Set Books 1-4
MOB Rescue Series Box Set Books 5-8
MOB Rescue Series Box Set Books 9-12

Much love,
Jovie

Also by Jovie

For the most up-to-date printable list of my sweet historical books:

Click here

or go to:

https://www.jografford.com/joviegracebooks

For the most up-to-date printable list of my sweet contemporary books:

Click here

or go to:

https://www.JoGrafford.com/books

About Jovie

Jovie Grace is an Amazon bestselling author of sweet and inspirational historical romance books full of faith, family, and second chances. She also writes sweet contemporary romance as Jo Grafford.

1.) Follow on Amazon!
amazon.com/author/jografford

2.) Join Cuppa Jo Readers!
https://www.facebook.com/groups/CuppaJoReaders

3.) Follow on Bookbub!
https://www.bookbub.com/authors/jo-grafford

4.) Follow on Instagram!
https://www.instagram.com/jografford/

Made in the USA
Las Vegas, NV
28 March 2024

87927880R00100